## OTHER WORKS BY DENENE MILLNER

*Act Like a Lady, Think Like a Man* (with Steve Harvey)

*Straight Talk, No Chaser* (with Steve Harvey)

*Dreamgirls*

*Hotlanta* (with Mitzi Miller)

*If Only You Knew: A Hotlanta Novel* (with Mitzi Miller)

*Hotlanta Book 3: What Goes Around* (with Mitzi Miller)

*The Vow: A Novel* (with Angela Burt-Murray and Mitzi Miller)

*A Love Story* (with Nick Chiles)

*In Love and War* (with Nick Chiles)

*The Angry Black Woman's Guide to Life*
(with Angela Burt-Murray and Mitzi Miller)

*Love Don't Live Here Any More* (with Nick Chiles)

*Money, Power, Respect: What Brothers Think, What Sistahs
Know About Commitment* (with Nick Chiles)

*The Sistahs' Rules: Secrets For Meeting,
Getting, and Keeping a Good Black Man
(Not to Be Confused with The Rules)*

# SPARKLE

## DENENE MILLNER

**SIMON &
SCHUSTER**

London · New York · Sydney · Toronto · New Delhi

A CBS COMPANY

First published in US by Atria, a division of Simon & Schuster UK Ltd, 2012
This edition published in Great Britain by Simon & Schuster UK Ltd, 2012
A CBS COMPANY

1 3 5 7 9 10 8 6 4 2

Simon & Schuster UK Ltd
1st Floor
222 Gray's Inn Road
London WC1X 8HB

www.simonandschuster.co.uk

Simon & Schuster Australia, Sydney
Simon & Schuster India, New Delhi

A CIP catalogue record for this book is available
from the British Library

ISBN: 978-1-47111-446-5
eBook ISBN: 978-1-47111-447-2

Typeset by M Rules
Printed and bound by CPI Group (UK) Ltd, Croydon, CR0 4YY

*For Whitney*

*Whose voice soared . . .*

*and set the standard . . .*

*and inspired . . .*

*and was loved.*

# SPARKLE

# CHAPTER 1

$S$ISTER WAS NEVER good at disguising what she was thinking. Not that she wanted to anyway. The way she narrowed her eyes, the way she twisted her lips, the placement of her hands, the shifting of her lithe, hourglass frame—all of it was her very deliberate way of letting anyone with eyes, ears and a half a brain cell know exactly what was on her mind. And right then, at that very moment, as she stood, hand on hip, in the kitchen of the Discovery Club, alternately glaring at the singer on the cramped, dilapidated stage and the audience's enthusiastic response to him, Sister's stance was screaming three things: *Troll! Damn, he can sing! You couldn't pay me to go out on that stage after him!*

Sparkle was fluent in Sister-speak—knew that she'd have to do some fast talking if she was going to get her big sister to walk out on that stage and perform behind Black, a big, greasy, sweaty mess of a man with a voice and stage presence that made him practically morph into Marvin

Gaye before the audience's eyes. Sister craved attention—fancied herself *the* star. Playing musical cleanup was not an option.

Sparkle's eyes shifted between Sister's glower and the stage, where, at that very moment, Black was whipping his hand in the air to signal the piano, bass and harmonica musicians to stop playing his soul-stirring blues tune. Black caressed the microphone between his fat, sweaty palms, closed his eyes, cocked his head and stood silent—a dramatic pause that suspended space and time and left the packed crowd hanging so hard on his next note that even the roaches crawling over the crusty dishes back in the kitchen stood still.

And just when the room was about to burst waiting to see what the theatrical singer would do next, just when the piano man's arms, suspended over his instrument's keys, started to ache, just when Sister shifted onto her other hip and furrowed her brow so hard her foundation yawned just a bit on her forehead, Black let go of the microphone on the stand, raised his hands in exaltation and, with a growl that rose from the depths of his belly, belted, "I'm a maaaaaaaan!"—the hook to the soul-stirring, make-'em-scream-hallelujah a capella version of Bo Diddley's smoky blues song.

Everybody—the musicians, the drug dealers sitting in the choice seats, the young guys cozying up to their dates with dreams of getting lucky later on, the shop workers and hairdressers and school cleaners who'd climbed out of their work clothes and into their finest outfits to enjoy what little bit of fun and freedom they could muster in the bowels of the club, the bartender, the waitresses—everybody jumped to their feet and hollered like they were sitting on the front pew testifying at the holiest of church revivals.

And Black? He grilled it up and ate it whole. Every. Single. Morsel.

Sparkle knew it was time for some fast talking, or she was going to lose Sister. "Sister, please, just hold on, now . . ." Sparkle began. But Sister was having none of it.

"No," she said simply, hand still on hip, eyes still on Black.

"But you're up next—I can't change the run of the show and if you don't go after him, you're not going to get to go at all," Sparkle reasoned.

"I said *no*," Sister snapped. "I am not going on after a troll who just sang himself cute."

Sparkle adjusted her angle so that she was standing in front of Sister, blocking her view of Black and the audience, which by now was shouting and clapping and testifying so hard the clapboard floors and crumbling wall plaster rumbled. "Pretty please?" Sparkle begged, turning on her modest-little-sister charm.

"I don't even know why I let you talk me into coming down here," Sister said, her eyes shifting from one young face to the next. The room was full of young'uns—their naiveté practically dripping from their pores. At twenty-eight years old, with enough living under her belt to out-match most fifty-year-olds, Sister had neither the time, the energy, nor the foolishness it would take to win over a bunch of teenagers anyway. "I think I'm the oldest sardine in this can."

"You don't look it," Sparkle quickly opined.

"That's the truth," Sister said slyly, flipping her hair and running her hands along the outlines of her hip-hugging satin pencil skirt and her tight black sweater with a scoop cut in the back. Sister looked good. And she knew it, for sure. "It's your song anyway. You go out there and sing it."

"But you're the singer in our family," Sparkle said, anxiously peeking over her shoulder and saying a silent prayer that Black keep milking the crowd long enough for her to con Sister onto the stage.

"So?" Sister snapped. "You can sing, too."

"Yeah," Sparkle said, moving herself into her sister's line of vision. "But you know how to keep people's attention . . ." Just as the words pushed themselves from Sparkle's lips, both she and Sister caught sight of him—some goofy guy with Coke-bottle glasses and an awkward grin, staring down Sister. "See?" Sparkle said quickly. "People want to see you talk. Imagine how you'll blow them away when you sing. Come on, Sister, just say you'll do it . . ."

Just then, Black sat on top of his final note, stretching it so far and so long and so wide the audience's thunderous applause was near deafening. When he finally let go of the note, he stood there in his black jumpsuit, a wash rag in his hand, mopping his brow and taking in every praise like it was a steak dinner. The announcer rushed to the stage, he, too, applauding wildly, and patted Black on the back while he expertly snatched the mic from the singer. "Black, ladies and gentlemen," the announcer said. "We'll keep the applause going. Next up . . ."

Sparkle's heart skipped two beats. "Please," she begged

Sister. She was racing against time. "I just want to hear my song."

The announcer kept on: "Sister Anderson! This is her first time at the Discovery Club, so make her feel welcome!"

Sparkle looked at the announcer, then back at Sister. She was starting to panic. "Please, I begged the owner to let you come sing tonight and he squeezed us in even though he really didn't want to. If you back out now, no one will ever hear my song and no one can sing it like you can. Now, I went over everything with the band, and . . ."

Just then, all 300-plus pounds of sweaty Black rolled their way to the backstage area, crowding out all those who stood waiting their turn to take the stage. He practically pushed Sparkle out of the way to step right in front of Sister; his hot breath seared the rouge Sister had swiped from the makeup case her mother had buried in the bathroom linen closet. Black stared Sister down as the announcer called her name once again. "You sure you want to do this?" he asked, a smug smile stretching across his face.

Sister couldn't stand smug bastards, but what she adored more than anything was a challenge. There was no way she was going to step back off this bet. Sister smiled back at Black, locked eyes with him, and, without saying a word, slipped her arms out of her sweater and spun it around so that the low cut was in the front, where there was now *lots* of cleavage. Sister, her eyes digging straight down into Black's soul, said everything that needed to be said between the two. Sister's smirk put the exclamation point on it.

Black swallowed hard and shifted his girth out of Sister's way as she stepped past him and sashayed onto the stage. And when she pulled the microphone close to her hot red lips, looked out over the packed crowd and said "thank you" for the opportunity to perform, there wasn't an eye in the house focused on anything other than Tammy "Sister" Anderson. Women crossed their legs and twisted a little in their seats and, out of the corner of their eyes, took stock of their men's reaction to the siren on the stage. The men—well, there were quite a few who turned up the bottoms of their cups of liquor and took long, hard swigs of their beer. Those who really didn't give a damn what their women thought of their actions or figured they had plenty of time to sweet-talk their ladies after disrespecting them made no bones about leaning in and running their eyes from the top of Sister's fine brown hair, across her ample bosom, past her invitingly curvy hips and thick, luscious legs and all the way down to the tips of the red toenails peeking from her high-heeled sandals. Sister was sexy. She knew it. And everybody else in the room knew it, too.

Sister winked at Sparkle as the band played the introduction to "Yes I Do," an upbeat, Motown-styled song Sparkle had scribbled in her dream journal just a few weekends earlier while she was keeping time with Mama at the dress shop. The words were sugary sweet and innocent, like the yarns of lace fabric Sparkle's mother expertly worked into a bridal gown for a teenage girl who was going to be walking down the aisle just a week shy of her twentieth birthday. Sparkle had seen the light in the young bride-to-be's eyes and melted just a little; here was this nineteen-year-old girl, barely out of high school, about to recite her marital vows with a real man, when Sparkle, who was the same age, hadn't even gotten her first kiss. And when that bride-to-be stepped in front of the mirror to admire herself in her wedding dress, Sparkle thought she was the luckiest girl in the world and that, surely, if a man kissed her and told her he loved her and asked her for his hand in marriage, she wouldn't hesitate to say, "Yes, I do."

In Sister's hands, though, the sweetness of the song took on a wholly different meaning. As she stood on that stage gyrating her hips and pouting through the words and running her hands through her hair and up and down her curves, "Yes, I do" was way less sweet, innocent bride-to-be.

"All right—we got that part down," Sister yelled into the mic as she pushed it back into the mic stand and smashed her hands together. "Now give me a soul clap!"

Sparkle could have jumped out of her skin. A soul clap? In the middle of the first verse? The audience had barely heard the song and Sister was encouraging them to stomp all over the words and the melody and her voice with a bunch of maniacal clapping? Horrified, Sparkle balled her fist as she waited for Sister to give her even the tiniest of glances; she was intent on giving her the "stop messing with my song" death eye—until, that is, she heard the audience cheer and fall right in line with the soul clap.

"Don't lose my beat. I need my beat," Sister demanded, leaning into the mic with a wry smile. She stalked the stage, her eyes sweeping every inch of the room, connecting with every gaze that met her own. "That's it," she purred. And just when the crowd jumped to its feet and Sister was sure she'd won them over, she jumped back into the song. The added touch with her vocals instantly picked up the energy in the song and the vibe in the room—so much so that even Sparkle couldn't deny that Sister's funkier version of her sweet song was where it was at. Sparkle joined in the soul clap as she checked out the crowd; her eyes locked in on one particular man—muscular, chocolate, beautiful— who, in the middle of the frenzy her sister had stirred up, was watching her watch the crowd. He smiled and nodded at Sparkle; Sparkle dropped her eyes and smiled back. But by the time she got the nerve to look at the handsome man again, he was gone.

Confused, Sparkle turned her attention back to the stage; the crowd was cheering "more!" as Sister took her bows and the announcer made his way to the mic. Of course, he nearly tripped over his own feet as he focused not on where he was going, but on Sister's tight skirt. Sister looked over at Sparkle and gave her a wink.

"Give it up for Sister Anderson," he said to her butt, rather than the audience. Sister played right into it, striking a model pose that made the crowd cheer harder. Sparkle shook her head; Sister winked at her and shifted her attention to Black, who was standing next to her in the wings of the stage. Sparkle stole a quick glance and was surprised to see the handsome man who'd been eyeing her standing practically next to her, chatting up Black. She leaned in just a little to eavesdrop on their conversation.

"So what do you think, Mr. Manager, we gonna do some business?" Black asked.

The man looked at Black's face, quickly shifted down

to his belly, and then back up to his face. "You got to lose some weight," he said, before turning his attention back to the stage, where the announcer, still staring at Sister's behind, apologized profusely for being so crass as to stare at a lady's posterior. Even with the apology, though, he was still looking.

"My belly helps me sing," Black insisted, trying to keep the man's attention.

"Look, TVs are getting bigger and clothes are getting smaller," he said matter-of-factly. "You were made for radio."

"Man, you cold," Black said.

Sparkle tried hard to contain her giggle. That *was* cold.

Sister stepped off the stage just as the announcer invited up a drummer from Harlem who was next to perform; she made a point of standing directly in front of Black, that same wry smile she'd given him before she took the stage sitting on her lips. Black smiled back and bowed his head, as if he were addressing the Queen of England. "Feminine . . ." Black began, his eyes slowing panning down to Sister's cleavage, "um, charm. Mandatory group participation. Nice touches. See you next week?"

Though she'd clearly made the audience that loved him eat right out of the palm of her hand, Black made sure she knew that their unspoken rivalry wasn't over. Not even by a stretch.

"Maybe," Sister shrugged. "Maybe not."

Sparkle inserted herself between the two and hugged her sister hard. "You were great!" she said. "But we have to go. We have five minutes to catch the last bus."

Sparkle pushed Sister's jacket into her chest and grabbed her arm. But her stride was broken by the handsome gentleman, who now was focused solely on Sister.

"Excuse me," he said confidently.

Sister dismissed him with a quickness. "I don't date younger men."

"No, I'm not . . ." the man began.

Sparkle heaved a heavy sigh. And here she was thinking the cute guy was angling for *her*. As usual, the moment they caught a gander of Sister, all chances of Sparkle getting the attention quickly disappeared. "I'm sorry," she said, grabbing her sister's hand, "but we have to go."

The man watched intently as the sisters headed out of the club. He looked back up to find Black smiling at him. "Bird in a hand," Black laughed.

The man stood silently.

"So, what'd you say your name was again, Mr. Manager? So I can be sure to look you up when I get big time?"

"Big time, huh?" the man said, staring at Black's belly again and then back at the door through which the two women had disappeared. "Yeah, you're gonna get big all right. I'm Jeremiah Warren, but my people call me Stix."


Sparkle paced back and forth in front of the tiny bus-stop bench, alternately looking at her watch and down the street. She said a silent prayer that the two hadn't missed the last bus home; they didn't have money for a cab and if they had to walk in their fancy shoes, they wouldn't make it home until the sun found its way to the sky—and Mama would be sitting right there in the living room, waiting for them with the Bible and her belt. Just the thought of getting caught sneaking back into the house made Sparkle shiver. She was pulling her jacket a little tighter around her neck when she saw the headlights of the bus headed toward them.

"Oh, thank God," she said.

Moments later, Sparkle was collapsing in the seat—relieved, exhausted, excited. She burst into a full-on giggle as the bus roared through the streets of downtown Detroit.

"What are you laughing about?" Sister asked, settling back into the seat.

"They loved my song," Sparkle practically cheered.

"They loved *me*," Sister corrected.

"Of course they did," Sparkle said gently, tossing a tender look in her sister's direction. Touched, Sister smiled at Sparkle. Her little sister was the only somebody who loved her unconditionally—who praised her talent consistently and, with every breath she took, made clear that she loved nothing more in the world than her big sister. Well, except for maybe her music.

"They loved you because you were singing my song," Sparkle deadpanned.

Sister laughed and playfully shoved her sister away.

"That was fun," Sparkle said, still giggling.

"Yes it was," Sister said, leaning her head into Sparkle's.

"Next time, though, get through the first verse and hook before you do your soul clap, because . . ."

Sister sat up and looked Sparkle dead in her eye. "Uh, Miss Thing, 'next time'?"

"Well, yeah, I have a lot more songs," Sparkle said mat-ter-of-factly.

"Well then you better get a lot more confidence and sing them yourself. Because slavery is over," Sister said.

It was a continuation of the lecture Sister had given Sparkle all the way to the club—one that began with her begging her sister to sneak out with her and perform, con-tinued as Sparkle and their half-sister, Dee, stashed Sis-ter's stage outfit into a bag, stopped only long enough for the two to slip out of Dee's bedroom window, and then picked up again as the sisters ran to the bus stop and got there just in time to catch the first thing smoking at the Discovery Club. For as long as she could remember, all Sparkle had ever known about her big sister was that she wanted to sing—that she wanted to see her name written in bold letters and surrounded by lights on the biggest marquees, that she dreamed of owning the stage and hav-ing fans rushing to shake her hand and take her picture and watch her on TV, maybe as she sat in Johnny Carson's chair on *The Tonight Show* or sang her heart out on Dick Clark's *American Bandstand*, just like Tina Turner and Diana Ross and the Supremes. But something changed when Sister went off to New York City in search of that fame and those bright lights. Sparkle couldn't get her to talk about what happened; all she knew was that her sister came back without anything but her suitcase and a heart full of broken dreams.

"Really? You're not going to sing anymore?" Sparkle questioned.

"No," Sister snapped. "Now assume the position."

Sparkle reluctantly positioned her body to block the view of their fellow passengers, giving her sister just enough room to wiggle out of her fancy sweater and skirt and into a simple top and pants. As Sister pulled the shirt over her head, a bright light caught Sparkle's eye. It was the marquee at the Fillmore Theater, shining bright with Marvin Gaye's name bold as could be in the center of it all. "One day," Sparkle said to herself, smiling.

Visions of superstardom were still flashing through Sparkle's mind as she and her sister, shoes in hand, cut through their neighbor's backyard and ran up to the side of the red brick Tudor standing tall and wide on their tree-lined street. Their neighborhood and home were beautiful—much too well-to-do to justify two women sneaking in the side door of their house in the middle of the night. These kinds of things didn't happen in their neck of the woods—and they certainly didn't happen on Emma Anderson's watch. Just the thought of getting caught by Mama sneaking into her house—or having to explain that they did it so that they could go sing secular soul music at that dive of a club in the middle of Detroit—made Sparkle's tail ache almost as much as it would if her mother got a hold of it. Terror didn't even begin to explain the emotion running through Sparkle's heart as she realized her mother's bedroom light was on.

She and Sister exchanged frightened glances before Sister tapped lightly on the door. Not even a beat after they knocked, Dee swung open the door and, holding her bathrobe closed to block out the cold, shuffled aside so her sisters could tumble into the house. "Y'all late . . . and she's up," Dee said, absentmindedly running her fingers over her curlers.

Sparkle and Sister walked softly through the door and quickly up the stairs, making it into Dee's room just as they heard their mother's footsteps in the hallway. She always had this stomp to her step—like she was mad and on her way to tell someone about it. Didn't matter where she was headed, who she was going to see or what she had to say at the moment, Emma's brisk walk and size 9s made clear she had something to say, and everybody better get to listening.

Sparkle, Sister and Dee dived into Dee's bed—shoes, street clothes and all—and quickly pulled the covers up to their chins, trying to muffle their laughter, with no success. Nanoseconds later, Emma tapped on the door and then walked through it. She never waited for an answer. As far as she was concerned, this was her house and she could walk in and out of every room she pleased. It didn't matter if you were ready for her to be there. She didn't care if you were sleeping, studying, praying or naked—if Emma Anderson had it in her mind to walk into her daughters' rooms, she sure as hell wasn't going to wait for permission.

"What are y'all doing in . . ." Mama began. Her eyes set on Dee's bed, where all three of her daughters lay, cuddling and smiling.

"My babies," she said, smiling. "But y'all don't love each other *that* much," she snapped. "Sparkle, Sister, curl your hair and get to bed. We have church in the morning."

And as quickly as she'd arrived, Mama was gone. A beat later, she came right back in and yelled some more:

"And Dolores, shut that window! My heater ain't on for the fun of it!"

And with that, Emma stomped on back down the hallway. Sparkle and Sister tried their best to muffle their giggles.

Dolores reeled back as she watched her fully clothed sisters tumble out of her bed. "Y'all heifers sneak out and *I* get fussed at?"

Of course, that made Sparkle and Sister laugh harder. Dolores didn't know what to do with her crazy sisters. So she just shook her head, closed her window and climbed back into her bed as they peeked out her door, checked to make sure the coast was clear and disappeared into the dark hallway, their muffled giggles rising above the din of the crickets screaming outside her window.

# CHAPTER 2

IT'S NOT LIKE Stix didn't know Jesus. He was raised in the church—had a mother who saw to it that he was in church school and service every Sunday, Bible study every Wednesday, revival on Saturday night and every other church function in between. He didn't mind the pomp and circumstance of it all—the dressing up, the shouting, the preacher's theatrics, the lakeside baptisms, the collection plates. But there was something about all of that fire-and-brimstone talk that made Stix feel uncertain about spending what seemed like every waking moment in a church pew in general and in front of his childhood pastor in particular. Pastor Cofield, minister at the St. John's Baptist Church his mother attended back in Kansas City, got off on reminding the congregation that they were headed straight to hell with a tank of gas if they even thought about veering off God's path. Dancing on a Saturday night? You're going to hell. Kissing a girl and lusting after a little more? You're going to hell. Don't tithe? Hell. Drink? Straight to hell. At

age nineteen, with hormones and passion and desire cours-
ing through his veins like hot fire and dreams of becoming
the next Leonard Chess or Berry Gordy dancing around in
his head, there was no room for Stix to disavow all that was
fun and good and right about music—and the way it made
people feel and move and love. Stix especially couldn't see
why God would see fit to give him the gift of good music
and a vision of how to become rich, famous and powerful,
only to have some backwoods, loud-mouthed, potbellied
preacher who was the biggest sinner of all telling him that
Satan feeds off the big dreams Stix had for himself. So Stix
left the church, against his mother's will. And later, he left
her house. He never looked back at either one.

How ironic, then, that all those years later, there he
was, sitting in the back pew of New Hope Baptist Church,
the biggest, oldest, holiest black church in Detroit, chasing the dream that forced him to leave all that he loved?
Stix tried his best to suppress his disgust with it all—the
pastor sitting up in the pulpit like a king on a throne, the
deaconesses sitting front and center, trying to look demure
but surely plotting over which one could draw the pastor's
attention over the others, the ushers bossing and shush-
ing anyone who even blinked hard. He gave himself five
minutes till after the choir made it to their perch before he
beat it out of there. He had one mission only: to see if Sister
Anderson was anywhere up in the mix.

Stix sat at attention when the huge mahogany doors
leading into the sanctuary opened and the organist began
playing the processional music. An army of choir singers,
clad in their church robes with Bibles and tambourines and

handkerchiefs in their hands, floated down the aisle, their voices lifted in praise. Stix trained his eye on every one of the faces—searching, his disappointment palpable every time his eyes fell on a light-skinned woman who looked like, but wasn't, who he'd come to see.

And then, finally, after what seemed like a month of Sundays, he saw her.

Stix tapped his cousin, Levi, on his leg. Levi, who'd come only because Stix promised him they wouldn't stay for the entire service and that when they left, he'd buy Levi lunch. He was practically sleeping when his cousin's tap aroused him. "Six churches, six Sundays and six dollars later, I find her," Stix whispered, as he jabbed his finger in Sister's direction.

Levi's eyes locked on Sister. He gave a wretched grin. "Man, that's who you've been talking about? That's Tammy Anderson," Levi said, never once breaking his gaze. "She got two fine sisters, too, and they all can sing."

"Is that right?" Stix asked, staring.

"But their mama is crazy," Levi said, his words piercing the air just as the choir found its seats, the pastor stepped to his podium and the church fell quiet.

An old woman dressed in her Sunday best and a church hat that spanned practically half the pew shushed the two, but she didn't need to: Stix didn't want to say another word. All he wanted to focus on was how he was going to convince Sister Anderson to let him be her manager.

Three hours, four songs, one forty-minute sermon and three collection plates later, Stix had it all figured out. And by the time Sister Anderson had made her way out of the massive church and into the bright, sunlit streets of downtown Detroit, Stix was ready to pounce. His target: Sparkle.

Stix waited for Sister's little sister to get just a few feet farther away from her mother and her friends before he pounced. "Hey there," he said, practically jumping in front of her. His smile was infectious; it made Sparkle nervous— in a good way.

"Shh," Sparkle insisted, her eyes darting to where her mother stood just a few yards away, laughing with her friends Sister Clora and Miss Waters. Mama wasn't looking—yet. But as usual, Miss Waters had her eagle eye on Sparkle and was leaning in just a bit to catch whatever bits of the conversation she could pick up, which made Sparkle even more nervous than talking to the handsome guy from the club. Sparkle shifted her focus back to Stix, making it obvious that the two were being watched.

Within a beat, Stix caught on. "Bible study is at your house this week, right?" Stix asked, working with a little intel he'd picked up from the church bulletin.

"Right," Sparkle said stiffly.

Stix tried not to laugh at how miserably she was failing at pretending she didn't know him and was genuinely interested in talking about studying The Word. "You know, you're really bad at this," he chuckled. "Just act natural." He reached out to shake her hand: "I'm Stix."

Thrown, Sparkle wrinkled her brow. What kind of name was *Stix*?

"I don't know you well enough to tell you my real name, so it's Stix," he added, only half kidding.

"Sparkle," she answered back.

"Touché," he said.

"No, that's my name," Sparkle said, frowning.

Stix tossed her a wicked smile. "Well then, I'll see you at Bible study, Sparkle," he tossed as he walked away, leaving her standing in his wake.

Sparkle tried to contain her smile but it was near impossible; she'd spent almost a month searching the faces of practically every dark-skinned man who crossed her path, hoping it was the man who'd caught her eye at the club. Mind you, she had no idea what she'd say if she ever ran into him; she had a million beautiful words scribbled in her journal and stored in her daydreams for occasions such as these, but actually talking to a man in an "I like you, we should get together" kind of way? The tragically shy Sparkle would just as soon melt into the earth rather than fumble her words and prove, without a shadow of doubt, that, at age nineteen, she was inexperienced and too chicken to talk to boys.

And then, of course, there was Mama, always making sure no man could so much as look at her daughter without incurring the wrath. Sparkle gave a slick side glance in her mother's direction and, just as she suspected, there was Mama with her best friend, Sara Waters, and the nosiest woman in the church, Sister Clora, staring her down and twisting their lips in Stix's direction.

"Who's that talking to my baby?" Mama snapped, staring at Sparkle.

"Nineteen ain't a baby anymore, Emma," Sara said wryly.

Emma shot the dagger eye at her buddy, but Miss Waters gave it right back to her. "No need in eyeballing me, I tell the truth," she said with conviction. "It's in my contract as your friend. And I'm telling you, you hold on too tight to this one, she'll be unmarried and back on your doorstep just like Sister."

Sara's words stung, but Emma tried her best not to show it. Sister's return to her house after an obviously disastrous attempt to make it on her own in New York City was a sore spot for her—and the talk of the church, despite Emma's insistence that everyone mind their business about it and stop asking her to air her family's dirty laundry for all to see and pick at. "It's just temporary," Emma said curtly.

"Uh huh. New York just spit her right on back out, huh?" Sara said.

Emma went in for the kill—the only way she knew how to get her best friend out of her business with a quickness. "How about you worry about marrying off your big-butt daughter and I'll worry about mine."

Sister Clora let out a little giggle as Sara prepared, then let go of, her quick dagger-like response. There was no way she could win this war of words, not with her daughter, aptly described by Emma, tumbling in their direction, with Sparkle fast on her heels.

"Mama, I need some money," Tune Ann said to Sara. "They selling plate dinners in the church basement and they're going fast."

Emma smirked, but held back her full-on guffaw; Sara cut her eyes at her best friend and warned her: "Don't. Just don't."

Emma paid her friend no nevermind; she fell out into hysterics as Sara walked off with Tune Ann, her butt jiggling all the way as the two disappeared back through the church doors. But it wasn't Tune Ann's big booty that she was thinking about. It was that boy, circling around her baby girl like a buzzard looking for the kill, that had her attention. And she had every intention of finding out his intentions—and keeping him far, far away from her Sparkle.

Of course, one would have thought that Emma knew by now that there was no keeping men away from pretty women—that much she knew firsthand. Which explains why no more than three days later, there was that boy again, sniffing around her daughter—right there in her own living room, with another rascal who looked every bit as mischievous and conniving as the first. When she found them standing on her stoop, Emma's first inclination was to tell them to get the hell on, but Stix introduced himself and Levi and announced the two were there for Bible study before she could spit the words off her tongue. And really, what good, Christian woman would turn away obvious sinners trying to get a little Jesus in them? When Stix extended his hand, Emma met it with a slow once-over and a look that made it crystal clear: *Watch it, mister. Don't start none, won't be none.* Levi, taking it all in, didn't bother opening his mouth.

"Hmph," Emma managed as she stepped aside and let the two in the door.

Stix squared his shoulders and took a long gulp. Not a whole lot of people made Stix nervous. But Emma made quick work of setting a tone that warned him he needed to bring his "A" game if he was ever going to have a shot at convincing Sister she should be the first singer on his roster. He'd already plotted it out with Levi: the cousin would keep Emma and the other daughters occupied while he cornered Sister and made his pitch. Of course, seeing as Levi was the biggest heathen Stix knew, the only way he could convince him to sit through Bible study less than a week after forcing him to sit through church service was to promise him he'd find a way to get Levi a little quality time with Sister. After all, a brother does have his needs, and Levi had been lusting for Sister from way back.

"How you doin', ma'am," Levi said, taking off his hat and giving Emma a short wave as he passed through the doorway. "Where's your daugh . . . I mean, where is Bible study?"

Stix balled his fist and cut Levi a nasty look.

"Back there in the living room," Emma said dryly. "Everyone's watching the color TV for an hour and then we're going to study the Bible. Follow me."

"Yes ma'am," Stix said as Levi took a gander of the fancy house. It was ornate and beautifully furnished, unlike any home he'd ever been in. Where he came from, most people—especially black people—didn't live in houses like Emma Anderson's. Not in 1968, in an all-white neighborhood. Levi knew Emma was a professional singer way back in the day, but rumor had it she couldn't cut it out there in the big time—not with the likes of artists like Aretha Franklin and Diana Ross and Tammi Terrell showing everybody how it's done. Some of what he'd heard even suggested that Emma Anderson came back to Detroit broke, with nothing but some tall tales of making it big in New York and three daughters nobody could account for.

But standing in the foyer of her house, Levi was pretty convinced that no matter what happened to Emma over there in New York, she'd done pretty all right for herself.

"Well, what you waiting for, a written invitation?" Emma snapped at Levi. "Time is ticking and we only have about ten more minutes before I shut off that TV and we get down to the Lord's work. If you want to watch a little before we get started, you better come on."

Levi and Stix jumped to attention and followed Emma into the living room, where a good number of people, mostly young folk, were crowded around the color TV set, watching *The Smothers Brothers Comedy Hour*. Satin Struthers, a famous black comedian whose anti-Negro rants about the Civil Rights Movement and its leaders made him the toast of white audiences everywhere, was mid-rant about how stupid black people are for rioting in their own neighborhoods. "I mean, I look at that foolishness on the TV, people running all around, grabbing TVs and liquor and shoes that don't even fit their feet and I say to myself, 'Self, you look black, but today, we gone be white. We giving up our black card.'"

A few of the people surrounding Emma's new Sony Trinitron color TV laughed hard at Satin as Emma directed Stix and Levi to the couch and took her seat next to the television. Sparkle caught Stix's eyes and he gave her a little smile in return, sending her heart into flutters.

Levi, who'd already surveyed everyone sitting in the room, didn't bother to sit down; he had some work to attend to. "Uh, excuse me, Ms. Anderson. Where is your bathroom?" he asked.

"Down the hall, second door on your right," Emma answered.

"Thank you, ma'am," he said, still holding his hat in his hand as he made his way down the hall. He wasn't headed for the bathroom, though. He headed toward the light, where he found Sister sitting near the open door of her bedroom—the third door on the left.

Leaning against the doorway, he let his eyes sweep across Sister and quickly decided that she was, without question, one of the prettiest women he'd ever seen. "You're not coming to Bible study?" he asked simply.

"Haven't you heard? I'm a heathen. Don't want to sit in there and be a hypocrite," Sister said sarcastically.

"Look at that. We already have something in common, because I only came here so I could ask you out," Levi said, giving her a smooth smile—one that Sister met in kind.

"The other door to the right," Emma snapped in Levi's ear, making him jump. Neither he nor Sister had heard her creeping down the hallway to see what the couple was up to.

Levi slowly turned to face Emma's icy stare and, without a word, disappeared into the bathroom. Emma tossed Sister one last look, rolled her eyes and headed back into the living room, only to find the entire room of teenagers leaning into the TV and staring so hard they hadn't noticed her standing in the middle of them all. On the television was the British rock band Cream, singing their hit song, "Sunshine of Your Love." All of them loved the song, but Sparkle was mesmerized by the band—their musicianship, the funk that sat on the groove of the melody, the beat. All of it. She wanted to know more about them—how they came up with the arrangement, who of the group was the one who came up with the lyrics, which came first, the music or the words. Musician to musician, she respected their art—for real.

Emma gave the room a once-over and quickly decided to stop the madness. "That's funky, huh?" she asked, snapping her fingers and doing a shimmy. "Makes you want to dance!"

Sparkle was horrified, but Dolores, never one to be embarrassed by much, was amused. "Get it, Mama!" she laughed, snapping her fingers and goading her on.

"Oh yeah, I'm going to get it. And you will, too," Emma said, shaking her hips. "Because you start off dancing and the next thing you know, you have a baby you can't feed."

The whole room giggled, but Emma made clear she wasn't fooling around.

"Uh huh. I know you don't believe me. But I can tell you when he said, 'I'll soon be with you, my love, to give you my dawn surprise,' he wasn't talking about making her French toast," Emma snapped.

Sparkle wasn't sure what to be more shocked about: that her mother was talking about sex in front of the entire Bible class or that she knew the words to Cream's song. Whichever, she wanted her mother to hush. She sat still and stared straight forward, willing herself not to look in Stix's direction out of fear that if she looked in his eyes, she'd die right there on Mama's gold, plastic-covered couch.

Stix paid Sparkle no mind; he laughed right along with the rest of them.

"I'm just telling you the truth," Emma continued. "This kind of music is going to lead you to a bad end. Now open up your Bibles," she snapped as she turned off the TV, eliciting groans from her young charges. "Hey now," she said, throwing up her hands for emphasis. "The deal was color television for an hour, then Bible study. I lived up to my end of the bargain, now it's your turn."

As everyone pulled out their Bibles, Sister sauntered into the room, with an almost annoyed look on her face. "Reverend Bryce is on the phone and says that he needs you to come check the books," she said out loud as if she were saying it to no one in particular, even though the message clearly was meant for her mother. "The numbers aren't adding up."

With not so much as a second's hesitation, Emma headed straight for her room. She hadn't heard the phone ring; surely, Pastor knew better than to call the house during Bible study, didn't he? When he knew Emma wouldn't be near the phone?

Sister watched her mother rush down the hallway and then turned the TV back on. She joined in with the crowd of Bible thumpers, gyrating her hips to "Sunshine of Your Love," and was giving everyone quite the show when Emma rushed back into the living room with her coat and purse.

"Oh no. All these hormones can't be in here unattended," she snapped as she turned off the TV. "Everybody out."

Emma's students all jumped to attention and grabbed their things with a quickness, filing out of the living room with great haste—all of them, that is, except Stix, who clearly was lingering. Sparkle hung back, too, hoping he'd say something—anything—to her. Still perched on the couch, she smiled at him awkwardly, hoping he'd get the message seeing as, as usual, she didn't know what the heck to say to him first. But Stix just shot her a corny smile—totally oblivious to the fact that she wanted him to talk to her. He was on a mission—a mission that really didn't have anything to do with the cute girl on the couch. It was the other sister he had his eye on.

Clear that Stix had no intention of chatting, Sparkle finally got up. "Well," she sighed, "good night."

"Um, yeah—good night," Stix said, giving a little wave as Sparkle slowly walked down the hall. She'd barely made it past the first door when Stix turned his attention to Sister, who, having watched the whole scene between her little sister and the handsome guy, just shook her head.

"What?" Stix said, confused by Sister's reaction.

Sister just left Stix standing there—and called out, "Why are all the cute ones stupid?" over her shoulder as she disappeared down the hall, too.

"Wait," Stix said, "I was hoping I could talk to you." He watched as the last few people headed out the door, then looked back at Sister, who, still, was paying him no mind. He ducked out of sight just in time when Emma took a last survey of the room; satisfied it was empty, she rushed out the door to meet the pastor, completely unaware that she'd left the all those hormones standing right there in her living room.

"Okay, girls, I'm gone. Sparkle, do the dishes. Dolores, study. Sister, pretend you're grateful to be back and clean something," she called out just before she shut the door behind her.

As soon as he heard the lock click in the doorjamb, Stix headed down the hallway in search of Sister—a mission that was quickly interrupted by a beautiful piano melody that stopped him in his tracks. Stix looked up as if he could sniff the music in the air; his nose lead him to a small room just off the living room, where he found Sparkle behind the keys of a black baby-grand piano, losing herself in a song about what it's like to have feelings for someone and not know what to do with them. "What can I do with this feeling, hooked on your love—sweet love, love," she purred, her eyes closed tight as her fingers caressed the piano keys.

Sparkle stopped playing and glanced down at the pages of her journal on the piano and, in her periphery, saw Stix standing—watching. "What are you doing here?" she asked, stunned.

"That was beautiful," Stix said simply.

Sparkle couldn't contain her excitement; she was happy to see him. She whipped off her glasses and absentmindedly smoothed her hair and adjusted her hot-pink button-up sweater—the one she'd spent hours fretting over, with the hopes that Stix would notice it when he came to Bible class. He hadn't.

"It still needs a lot of work," Sparkle said of her song as she glanced at the journal page with the lyrics. Scribbled at the top in bubble letters and hearts were the words "Hooked on Your Love," the title she'd settled on for the ditty, which she'd dreamed up just that past Sunday, just moments after she watched Stix walk away from the church—from her.

"Wait, that's *your* song?" Stix asked, surprised. "You wrote that?"

"Only if you thought it was good," Sparkle said quickly.

"It's phenomenal," Stix said without hesitating.

"Then I wrote it," Sparkle said, without missing a beat.

They both laughed. For the first time since she'd laid eyes on Stix, she felt comfortable around him, but it was of no surprise; there were a lot of things that made Sparkle uneasy—talking to boys, singing in front of a crowd, her mother—but talking about music smoothed her out like nothing else, even if the person she was speaking to was the man who left her tongue-tied for weeks.

"Did you write the song your sister sang at the Discovery Club a few weeks back?" Stix asked.

"Yeah," Sparkle said. "Sister kind of made it her own, but . . ."

"Wait a minute, wait a minute," Stix exclaimed, clapping his hands together and rubbing them like he was about to sit down to a fine southern-fried chicken meal. "You wrote that song? You wrote the one you were just singing? And you wrote the ones in here?" he demanded, running around the piano and looking in her journal.

Sparkle closed her journal. "Yes," she said. "I wrote it all."

"What are you guys doing with your music?" he asked.

"Nothing," Sparkle deadpanned.

"Well, why not?" Stix demanded.

"Because my mom would never let me," Sparkle said slowly. "Plus, I'm not the singer in the family. Sister is.

Then Dee. I just sing in the choir because I don't want to sit by myself in church . . ."

"No offense," Stix said, cutting off Sparkle, "but I'm just hearing a bunch of excuses."

"Excuse me?" Sparkle said, offended.

"I don't mean to be rude," he said, trying to get a handle on his tone. Stix realized that not everyone could handle his directness. It was something he was working on. "I'm passionate. Especially when it comes to music. That's why I'm here." Stix sat on the piano bench next to Sparkle; the heat from his body made her tingle a little—enough for her to consciously will herself not to tremble. Or faint. "I'm staying with my cousin Levi," Stix said. "I'm from Kansas City. We have a nice jazz scene down there, and I was managing a few acts around town, but the money is in Motown. I want to be the next Berry Gordy. I figured his stomach doesn't growl like mine anymore and maybe he's leaving a lot of steak and potatoes out there."

Sparkle giggled. "You're making me hungry."

Stix laughed with her. "Do you mind if I hear the song again?" he asked.

"I've never really performed for anybody," Sparkle said nervously.

Just then, Dolores and Sister and her attitude walked into the room, startling the two. "What are you doing here?" Sister demanded.

Stix looked the two of them over and, instantly, he saw the vision: Sister and The Sisters. "Does she know the song?" he asked Sparkle, pointing at Sister.

"I don't tap dance for nobody," Sister insisted. "Besides, I'm a model."

Dolores didn't even bother holding back her laughter at that one.

"What?" Sister asked, annoyed.

"You have to be *paid* to model in order to be called a model," Dolores said, refusing to give her sister even an inch. She was good for that—didn't have a problem telling Sister about herself and saying exactly the first thing to come to her mind, without a care in the world about its biting effects. Part of it was about jealousy; Dolores wasn't bothered by the fact that everyone treated Sister like her light skin and fine hair made her God's gift, but it ticked her off to no end that she, with her milk-chocolate skin and coarse, curly hair, was automatically relegated to "the Ugly Sister" status. Even more, though, it bothered Dolores that Sister squandered her life depending on her beauty to get over—to tragic results. And so Dolores reminded Sister of these things as often, it seemed, as she breathed.

Sister gave it back to her all the same. "You're just mad because your hair is nappy," Sister snapped.

"You guys, don't do this," Sparkle pleaded, trying to bring order between her sisters, who were acting in front of company like they were anything but blood.

Dolores couldn't resist. "I'd rather have nappy hair and a brain than have to depend on what's between my legs to survive," she snapped.

Without warning, Sister lunged after Dolores and in moments they were swinging wildly at one another like they were mortal enemies. It was comical enough to Stix that he started laughing, but Sparkle didn't find the fights between her sisters at all funny. "Don't laugh, help me!" she pleaded to him, grateful that at least this time, she'd have some help breaking up the two before someone got hurt. "Stop it!" she yelled as the two of them pulled the girls apart.

"Come on," Stix insisted. "You guys are sisters. Act like it! Now Dolores, you apologize to her."

Dolores reeled back, disgusted: "Man, I don't even know you, and you trying to tell me . . ."

"Just do it and save your lip," Stix ordered.

"She got a lot of that," Sister swiped.

"Hey," Stix said to Sister, "just because you're light and bright don't make you right. Your sister is beautiful. All of you are. And you have something special. Something real special. You're fighting and you should be together, singing, making music. Girl groups are hotter than ever right now. You could take over and you're up here tearing each other down."

The sisters—each of them—absorbed his words, for different reasons, mind you. Just as easily as Stix envisioned masterminding his own superstar girl group, Sister could see herself finally having a shot at stardom, Dolores was counting the stacks of money she could make to put toward tuition at medical school and Sparkle, well, she wanted nothing more than to have her songs performed in front of legions of people—to become one of the most respected songwriters of her time.

Stix interrupted all of their fantasies. "Now kiss and

make up," he said slyly, lowering his eyes and licking his lips a little.

"Ugh," Sister snapped. "Men always turn everything into sex."

"You would know," Dolores said. She couldn't help herself. Everyone cut her a look. "Okay, okay," she sighed. "I'm sorry. You just leave yourself wide open . . . oh God, I did it again."

Sparkle slapped her hand over Dee's mouth and shook her head as the four laughed. Their giggles came to a quick halt when they heard the front door slam.

Mama was home.

Sheer terror struck everyone in the room. Sparkle, the most scared of all, didn't even bother saying anything; she just marched over to the nearest window, her palm on Stix's massive back, opened it and ordered the man out.

"But I'm going to get hurt . . ."

Sparkle didn't say a word—just pushed. Stix fell out of the window just as Emma entered the piano room to find Sparkle and Dee sitting at the piano and Sister standing over them.

Emma didn't even bother saying "hello"—just went straight to the orders. As usual. "Dolores, I figured if you can do calculus, you can balance the church's books. Come on, get your coat."

The open window caught Emma's eye; when she walked over to it, Sparkle was sure she was going to faint.

"What is it with you girls letting out my heat?" she said, disgusted, as she closed the window. Clearly, she wasn't expecting an answer; she just turned around and walked out, Dolores fast on her heels. "My house isn't clean!" she yelled from the front door. "I want it clean when I get back."

It wasn't until they heard the front door close that Sparkle and Sister took another breath. Without saying a word, the two headed to Sparkle's room. Well, really, it was both Sparkle and Sister's room, seeing as the elder of the two had recently taken up residence there. From the looks of it, Sister didn't expect to be staying long.

"Why won't you unpack?" Sparkle asked as she twirled into her bed and watched Sister pull her brush out of her suitcase, one of three bags that still held her clothes, despite that she'd moved back into their mother's home almost a month ago.

Sister didn't answer. Instead, she tossed her brush back into her toiletry bag and pulled her treasured music box close to her. She wound it up and watched as the black ballerina twirled to the tinkling melody. It soothed her, that sound—sweet, innocent, pure. Precious. That was what her mother called her when she gave it to her many Christmases ago. When, in a small glimmer of decency, Mama had pulled herself together just enough to remember that the holiday called for gifts and that children loved those gifts and that she had daughters who would love to unwrap presents on Christmas morning, too. Sister hadn't been expecting anything; back then, her mother barely remembered to keep a gallon of milk in the refrigerator so that the girls didn't have to eat their cereal with water. But when she woke up that Christmas morning and found that music box sitting on the kitchen table—no wrapping, just a bow—and she heard the song and saw the black ballerina dancing, she knew that somewhere deep down inside, there was love in her mother's heart. Love for her little girl.

"If you want, I'll move in with Dolores so you can have your room back," Sparkle said, interrupting Sister's memories.

"No," she said quickly. "I really don't plan on being here that long."

"You said that two months ago," Sparkle said practically under her breath. Instantly, she wished she could call the words back. Sparkle certainly didn't want her sister to think she wanted her to leave, or that she was keeping count of how long she'd stuck around. She admired Sister. She just wanted her to stay, to get herself together and be a part of their family again.

Sister heard Sparkle's jab—and it stung. But she saved her words. Instead, she turned out the light and climbed into bed with her baby sister.

"I'm sorry," said Sparkle.

"Don't ever be sorry for telling the truth, Spark," Sister said, settling into her pillow.

"Why won't you tell me about New York?" Sparkle said, turning toward her sister.

"Good night, Spark," Sister snapped.

Sparkle knew not to push. "Good night," she said simply.

And then something tapped on the window—hard. Sparkle jumped: "Did you hear that?" she asked, scared.

Both of the girls jumped up, scrambled to the window and peeked through the curtains. There was the sound again—a pebble banging against the glass. And there was Stix.

Sister sucked her teeth. "Your Romeo is out there," she said as she climbed back into the bed.

Sparkle opened the window and tossed Stix a frown, even as she blushed at the sight of him. "You can't come throwing rocks at my window. You know my mother has a gun."

"There's an underground club tonight," Stix said, undeterred by the quick image of Emma chasing him down the street. "The kind songwriters don't want to miss. You have to hear the music they play—stuff that's not making it on the radio. Come with me."

Sparkle replaced her furrowed brow with a look of worry. Stix pushed harder: "I promise, I'll get you back home safe and sound."

Sparkle pulled her head back from the curtain. "He wants me to go hear music with him," she said to Sister— excited but scared to accept his invitation.

"You've snuck out of the house for less," Sister said lazily as she climbed out of the bed and headed to her suitcase. "Tell him to meet you at the side door in ten minutes. I think I can work a small miracle by then," she said, pulling a red dress, a tube of lipstick and her brush from her suitcase.

Sparkle's eyes grew wide.

Her heart, wider.

# CHAPTER 3

THE MUSIC WAS loud, the room dark and sweaty. And everywhere Sparkle's eyes landed, there was another young couple, hugging and kissing and grinding—their hips, lips, hands and feet dragging to the rhythm of the songs. Sparkle had never seen anything like this—couldn't wrap her mind around how so many other teens managed to escape the confines of their parents' homes, make their way to this dark little hole in the middle of the night and, without a care in the world about who was watching, engage in an intimate, sexually charged dance that would make Jesus question whether they were worthy of walking through the pearly gates. Desperate not to come off as a prude in front of Stix, Sparkle tried to hide just how uneasy and out of place it all made her feel, but when Stix took her hand, led her to the middle of the dance floor and pulled her hips toward his, her tightness made clear that her shyness was getting the best of her.

"I'm not going to bite," Stix said, leaning into Sparkle's

ear so she could hear his voice over the din of the dance floor. His eyes sent a different message, though, as they traced the lines of Sparkle's tight red dress hugging her Coke-bottle figure, Stix was sending the signal that if she were on the menu, he would devour her.

"How do I know that?" Sparkle asked, trying to sound cool, grown-up.

"Guess you're just going to have to trust me," he said, peering into her eyes. He gently pulled Sparkle's body against his and swayed as his hands sat on the small of her back. Instantly, she found his rhythm—and let go.

"Yeah, that's it," Stix smiled. "You feel that bass? You hear that melody? It's digging down into your soul, isn't it?"

Sparkle, consumed with trying not to faint at the mere thought of dancing in Stix's arms, hadn't even considered the music until he pointed it out. The song was incredible—clearly influenced by Motown, but with a rawness that made it gritty, a little dirty. "Make you say yes," the singer sang, channeling Otis Redding. "I'm going to make you say yes."

"What is this?" Sparkle asked, the music taking over her body. "I've never heard this one before."

"I know," Stix said simply. "A lot of the music they play here is recorded by musicians and singers and songwriters trying to get discovered. Recording executives slip in here from time to time to hear it—see what the real audience is digging. You're not going to hear the stuff they play over and over again on the radio or what Dick Clark is pushing on *American Bandstand*. This right here is where music comes to find life. It's where real people find real music."

Sparkle closed her eyes, zoned in on the melody and

let her body fall into the groove. The chord changes were intricate—beautifully woven over the powerful bass line and backed up with a killer snare. Whoever put the song together knew what he was doing.

"They showcase music here every Wednesday night," Stix said. He could feel Sparkle's body loosen beneath his fingertips. "Maybe one of these days, you can get some of your music blasting through these here speakers."

Sparkle stared into Stix's eyes. "You really think so?" she asked. "You think my music would play here?"

Stix smiled and pulled Sparkle closer. "Yeah, I do," he said in her ear—gently, sultrily.

Sparkle felt it—that tingle she got whenever this man came her way. Except this time, the sensation didn't make her want to run; it made her want to hold on a little tighter.

And so she did.

Sparkle and Stix talked and laughed and danced—their common love of music the magic that intertwined the two. For hours, they listened closely to the artistry of the song-writers, musicians and singers—held them up to the light and examined every note, every lyric, every beat, as if their very lives depended on understanding the choices that were made in crafting the songs. When they weren't argu-ing the songs' merits, the two were holed up in a corner, eyes closed, ears attuned, just listening. Watching. Enjoy-ing. Drinking in the crowd's reactions—watching what got the people excited, what made them go scrambling off the dance floor and over to the bar, what made them press their bodies together just a little harder until two people were one writhing, sweaty, sensual mass.

This—this was what Sparkle lived for. And Stix, too. Music was as natural and necessary to the two as was breathing air.

Two hours later, Sparkle and Stix poured out of the club drenched from dancing up a sweat so intense, so searing, that when they stepped out into the cold air, steam rose from their bodies and heads. They cracked up at the sight.

"I'd better dry you off before getting you home," he smiled, reaching for her hand.

Sparkle placed hers in his palm and grinned as Stix pulled the keys to his motorcycle out of his pocket and climbed on. Careful to look as much like a lady as one could while hiking herself onto a motorcycle in a tight red dress, Sparkle climbed gingerly behind him. But just as when they'd rode to the club, she was uncomfortable pressing her body against his and wrapping her hands around his waist. No matter that they'd danced so suggestively inside the club; outside, when it was just the two of them, felt . . . different.

Stix noticed the hesitancy but didn't press it. He just revved the engine and took off into the night—let the wind wash over their faces as the thriving downtown scene unfolded before their eyes. Sparkle caught a glimpse of her and Stix's reflection in the rearview mirror and loved what she saw. They looked good together. And she smiled at the thought of the two of them being more than just friends who enjoyed listening to music. She wanted more. And for the first time in her young life, she'd found a man who wanted her, too.

A smile crept across Sparkle's face—and Stix's. And as the dark, open road rushed beneath his Triumph, Sparkle snuggled closer—squeezed Stix tighter—and knew in her heart, for sure, that he was all her own.

By the time they arrived at Sparkle's block, it was late—the kind of late when you don't want to let go of a magical night. Stix parked his motorcycle just a few houses down from Sparkle's place and, after helping her climb off, laid his jacket on the curb so that she could sit next to him. He didn't want the night to end, either.

"So did you have a good time?" he asked.

Sparkle looked down at her lap and picked off an imaginary piece of lint. "Yes, I did," she offered. "Thank you for taking me."

"Anytime," he said. "Stick with me and I'll take you plenty more places—I can show you some things."

Sparkle willed herself to say something; right there, right then, being shy was not an option. "What can you show me?"

"Lots," Stix said. "Like, take for instance, how to write a good lyric . . ." he began.

Sparkle reeled back. *Huh?*

"I think your lyrics are too safe. Unlike the music we heard tonight. You dug it because it was in-your-face, real, telling you the truth," Stix continued, oblivious to how taken aback Sparkle was by his words. Clearly, they were thinking and talking about two different things. "Times are changing. I don't think the metaphorical lyrics are going to fly anymore."

Sparkle wrinkled her nose.

"You were impressed by my big word, weren't you?"

"I was," Sparkle said, smiling.

"In the spirit of telling the truth, may I tell you another truth?"

"I wouldn't want you to lie to me," Sparkle said, genuinely.

"Then why do you lie to yourself? About not wanting to sing? If you're writing these songs and you can sing, why aren't you singing them?" Stix demanded.

"I'm no Diana or Aretha," Sparkle said, looking down at her hands so that she didn't have to look Stix in his face.

"You're right," Stix said, without missing a beat. "You're Sparkle."

She also was Emma Anderson's daughter—a product of a woman whose dalliance in the music industry almost cost her and her daughters their lives. Singing professionally wasn't an option—wasn't going to be, ever. Stix wasn't from Detroit, so maybe he wasn't privy to the stories—didn't know the shame of it all. How it all played out in front of the fans and the neighbors and the church folk. Emma's daughters. Yes, music was the beat to Sparkle's heart, but her mother's failure was the rope that bound her—that assured that she, Dolores, even Sister, would never find peace if they put all their hopes into being stars. Failure was inevitable.

"Look," Sparkle sighed. "My mother used to sing professionally. She tried to break out on her own and it almost killed her. So thank you, but I know the realities of this business. I'm just doing this for fun."

"'So thank you, I know the realities . . .'" Stix snapped in a mocking tone.

"Hey! Stop it!" Sparkle demanded, pushing him in the arm.

"You first. What are you afraid of? Your mama or your

own voice?" Stix said. Sparkle's reaction made clear he'd
hit a nerve. "Okay, maybe you'll be just like your mother
and never reach your goal, but don't fall short of it because
you can't even admit you want it."

To this day, Sparkle couldn't tell you what came over
her at just that moment, but she couldn't stop herself from
blurting it out—from saying it out loud. "Okay, I want to be
better than Diana. I want to be a star."

It felt scary and exhilarating at the same time to say out
loud what she'd been screaming to herself from the moment her fingers touched a piano key at age eleven. Embarrassed, she laughed, and quickly did some backspinning.
"But you don't say that in this town because you end up
sounding like everyone else."

"Only if you believe you're like everyone else," Stix insisted.

Sparkle thought about what he said and decided that
she liked him. A lot.

Just then, a car passed by, reminding Sparkle of the
time. She had to get into the house—it was late. She rose,
and so did Stix.

"Thank you. I had a great time tonight. And in case I
never make it back out of the house," she said, giving a
nervous look to her home two doors down, "thank you for
making me tell the truth."

"You're welcome," he said.

The two stood in awkward silence, unsure of what to
do next. Sparkle thought for sure that she was going to melt
into the concrete if this man kissed her. Surely, she'd die
if he didn't. But she didn't know what to do—how to calm

herself while she waited for what was to come next, melt-
ing or death. And just when she couldn't take it anymore,
he leaned in and pressed his thick, soft lips against hers.

Her first kiss—everything she imagined it would be:
scary, exhilarating, sweet.

Stix looked lovingly into Sparkle's eyes as he tenderly
broke the kiss. "Can I make you a star?"

"What?" Sparkle said between heavy, laborious breaths.

"Do you want to be a star?" Stix asked again, this time,
more forcefully.

"Yes," Sparkle said, smiling. "I want to be a star."

"I don't believe you. Say it again!" he demanded.

Sparkle giggled. "Yes, I want to be a star."

"Okay, the first thing you have to do is write another
song for your sister . . ." Stix began. Sparkle's smile slipped
from her face, but Stix didn't notice. "Something where
she can work the crowd. And you have to get over your
fear of singing, because you and Dee have to back her up.
Everybody loves a good girl group."

Sparkle's eyes narrowed like slits. How was it possible that this man made her feel so high and so low in the
span of ten seconds? The stake he'd just driven through
her heart hurt like hell, but Stix was too focused on getting
what he wanted to notice. As usual.

"Of course, you're going to tweak your lyrics," he continued, oblivious. "Make them raw, more relatable." He
slapped his hands together and got giddy: "Fillmore Theater here we come! But first, you have to win Cliff Bell's."

"Cliff Bell's?" Sparkle asked, incredulous. "You have to
be invited to compete in their talent contests," she added

as she envisioned the popular lounge where only the best graced the stage. Sister, Dolores and Sparkle up there on that stage in their simple dresses singing their simple harmonies in front of the top music executives and talent show coordinators in Detroit? No. Way.

"I'll work on that," Stix continued, still oblivious. "Then after we win Cliff Bell's, we book more gigs, we meet Mr. Gordy and boom—you get a record deal."

Sparkle folded her arms. "You got it all figured out."

"Yep," Stix said confidently. "Now you go get your sisters and I'll go get Cliff Bell's."

"And you'll be our manager?" she asked.

"Yep."

"Then you manage to get my sisters," Sparkle said, looking Stix up and down and turning to walk away.

Stix grabbed her hand. "Do I have *you*?"

"I'm backup, remember?" she said, disgusted. "So it doesn't really matter until you get Sister. Good night."

And with that, Sparkle turned on her heels and took off toward her house, refusing to look back.

Flummoxed, Stix watched Sparkle walk away, but he wasn't moved enough by her anger to stop her. He watched as she took off her shoes and disappeared down the block, hoping, still, that he'd gotten through to her. Stix had big plans for Sister and her sisters. All he had to do was make them envision the success and put it to work to make their dream—his dream—a reality.

# CHAPTER 4

HE WAS BROKE as hell. Lived in a little shack—calling it an apartment was generous—over in the Twelfth Street neighborhood with all the other broke-as-hell Negroes. His job status was questionable. And he was from Kansas City, which meant he was country, too. But there was Sister, sitting across the table from Levi Warren at Lafayette's in Coney Island in downtown Detroit, sipping on a root beer float and talking about nothing in particular. It beat sitting up in Mama's house, waiting for orders or, even worse, waiting for her to toss another judgmental look in her direction. Sister accepted Levi's offer to go to dinner and the movies not because she liked him, really. He was just something—rather, someone—else to do. Plus, he wouldn't stop asking. So, there they were.

"How did you like the movie?" Levi asked as he swirled his straw in the murky float and used it to put a little whipped cream on his tongue.

"Who doesn't like Sidney Poitier?" Sister asked lazily.

"But next time you talk about picking someone up, make sure you have a car."

"I'm saving up for the right one," Levi countered quickly.

"I mean, how you call yourself picking up someone for a date and don't have a car, Levi?" Sister asked, shuddering as she remembered her mother's face when Levi told her he had no choice but to have Sister back at a decent hour because the buses stopped running after 11 PM where he lived in Twelfth Street. "Oh," Emma said, slipping a sly look in Sister's direction, "you don't have a car, huh? That's . . . interesting." Then, turning to Sister, Emma added: "Typical."

Sister chuckled to herself. "Taking me out on a date on a bus," she snapped. "Lucky I like you," she added, pulling a pack of cigarettes out of her purse and lighting one up.

Well, let's just say she was warming up to him. Really, she had no other choice. Levi's cousin, Stix, had practically attached himself to Sparkle's hip, which meant that everywhere Sparkle and Stix were, there was Levi, waiting for his chance to get in Sister's face. He was even going to church on Sundays—well, kind of. He and Stix had started showing up toward the end of the services and taking up residence in the back row so that Stix could have a crack at convincing Sister, Sparkle and Dolores to form a singing group that he would manage, and that past Sunday, both Stix and Levi made their move. Sister's first inclination was to tell the two of them to get on with all of that, but, well, let's just say the cousins had game.

"Cliff Bell's?" Sister had said, recoiling at the taste of the words on her tongue when Stix, Levi hot on his heels, made his way into the choir room to make his pitch. "I'm not getting up there embarrassing myself. And didn't Marvin get booed out of there?"

"It made him better," Stix said, without missing a beat. "And now he's traveling the world and making millions."

"You mean, Mr. Gordy is making millions," Sister snapped. She was all-too-familiar with how "managers" and "owners" operated: the ones with the pretty faces did all the work, and the men—well, they gave orders, kept the money and, when they got what they wanted or their pretty face decided she needed better, wanted better, they just found another pretty face.

"However much Marvin Gaye is making, it's enough to get him out of his mama's house."

The look on Sister's face said it all: that stung. "You don't have to be rude about it," Sister snapped, backing Stix down. Dolores came to his rescue. Kind of.

"I don't really know if you were asking me," she interrupted. "You never really looked my way, so our eyes never got to dance, but I'm in. Just to be clear, I'm in it for the money. Medical school is expensive, so no, you won't be getting twenty percent. Fifteen, max. When I get accepted into Meharry Medical School, you will have to replace me." Stix furrowed his brow and Levi chuckled and shook his head, but that didn't stop Dolores or her mission. "And if you pretend I don't exist going forward, I will turn my sisters against you. Other than that, sounds like fun!"

Confused, Stix shook his head; Levi chuckled. Sister glanced over at Sparkle, who got up abruptly from her

chair and headed for the door. "I'll wait for you guys outside," she said.

"I'll let you know," Sister said tentatively, her eyes following Sparkle toward the door. "My first day at Hudson's
is tomorrow."

Stix shot a look at Levi and back at Sister. "Working at
a department store? That ain't going to make you no . . ."
Stix started.

"Whoa, hold up now," Levi interrupted. "Tammy Anderson gotta eat. You can't keep a figure like that without
some solid meals, that's for sure."

Stix huffed.

"And I know I'd buy anything you were selling," Levi
added.

"Fine, Hudson's. But let me know about Cliff Bell's
soon," Stix said as he walked briskly to the door.

Levi hung back, though—knew instinctively that Stix
needed a few minutes of alone time with Sparkle. With
that, he was fine; though Levi couldn't stand being in that
church alcove, he sure didn't mind having a little alone
time with Sister. He'd lusted after this woman for years—
back before she went away to New York to pursue her passion as a model. She was fine. Still was, in Levi's book, but
back then? Levi counted her as the finest woman in Detroit.
She was good for using it to her advantage, too; it was nothing for her to be seen around town at the hottest night-
clubs, surrounded by men who were quick to buy drinks
and dinner for the young model who had found a small
measure of success modeling in local fashion shows and
even a few Ebony Fashion Fair shows in Chicago. People

thought she'd found success because of who her mother
was: Emma Anderson, a soulful singer who'd acquired her
voice in the choir stands of Antioch Baptist Church but lost
it chasing secular dreams of being a famous torch singer,
and had enjoyed quite a bit of fame locally and even found
a small national fan base for her music before her career
met a tragic end. When she finally crawled back to Detroit,
Emma had three daughters in tow, each one beautiful, by
two different men she'd sung background for in Harlem.
Tammy, the oldest, was the one everyone watched—the
one the men pined for. Back then, you had to come with
bank and game to get her attention. But now that she'd
lived—now that she knew what it meant to be at her high-
est and how hard the fall was to her lowest, Sister wasn't as
picky. Tammy Anderson, Levi figured, could be had. Even
by a man with nothing more than a dream.

"You know, you and I go together," he whispered in
Sister's ear.

Sister rolled her eyes and shot a look at Dolores, who
just shrugged her shoulders and went back to hanging up
her choir robe.

"We'd look good together in my ride. We'd look good
together at the movies. We'd look good together having dinner, holding hands, introducing ourselves as a couple . . ."

"Look, I know what you want, and it ain't to hold my
hand," Sister snapped.

"See, that's where you're wrong," Levi said. "I mean,
you're right about me wanting to do more than just hold
hands, but if that's all you're willing to let me have, I'll take
it. Why don't you let me do that for you?"

"Do what, Levi?" Sister asked, exasperated.

"Let me take you out. I'll come by and pick you up, we'll go see that new Sidney Poitier movie, get a little something to eat—all of that. Let me do that for you."

Sister shrugged. "Sure, I'll let you spend your money on me. But that's all I'm going to let you do," she said. "Now get on out of here. This here place is for choir members only. And you sure ain't no choirboy, Levi."

"You're right about that," he said as he backed out of the room. "I'm going to come get you. Be ready."

Sister snapped herself out of her thoughts about that day when the waiter delivered their food—two hot dogs with the works and an order of cheese fries to share. Any other guy who showed up at her doorstep talking about going on dates on the bus would have been quickly dismissed. But there was something about that Levi, Sister decided. Something she thought she might like.

"Look," Levi said. "I don't know how else to be than myself. I'm a straight shooter. I like you and I want to be your man."

Sister reeled back and laughed at Levi. Honestly? If she had a dollar for every time some man told her that one, she'd have enough to move out of Mama's house, find her own place in the white part of town, retire and have some cash left over for her children's children. Men were always feeding her lines, talking about, "Baby, you so fine—I want to be with you forever," and "Baby, I want to be your man— I'll take good care of you." But when it came down to it, they all wanted the same things: to sleep with her. To beat her. To own her. And to leave her.

They never wanted love.

"I'm not like all the other guys who just want to do you," he said. His words threw Sister off; it was as if he had repeated out loud what she'd just tossed around in her mind. Except he was focused on the most sordid details. "I heard about your reputation, even before you went to New York. But I think it's what guys say when they see something so beautiful and they know they can't have it—it's easier to make it something they wouldn't want by trying to tear it down."

Sister looked away, but she was still listening. She wasn't buying what he had to say just yet, but it did sound . . . different. Levi was giving it to her straight—skipping over the "I'm telling you what you want to hear to get what I want" part and getting down to the meat of the matter.

"I see your beauty, Tammy—inside and out. And I want to earn it, kind of like a job. So just tell me what you need to fall in love with me, I'll do it. 'Cause really, whether you believe me or not, I'm already in love with you."

*Love?* Sister thought to herself. Now, that was new. Of all the men she'd ever loved, of all the men who'd claimed they wanted her, no one had ever bothered to use that word with her. Hell, her own mother didn't tell her she loved her. Sparkle was the only somebody who ever said it, and Sister knew she truly meant it.

Sister took a drag on her cigarette and looked up at Levi—stared at him hard. "I've heard so much, it all sounds like BS to me," she snapped.

A smile slowly spread across Levi's face. "I better roll up my sleeves a little higher, then," he said.

"Hopefully not as high as your pants," Sister said, looking down at Levi's pants, which sat so high up on his leg she could see the his dark brown dress socks.

"That's the style," Levi insisted.

"Change it," Sister frowned.

They both laughed as Sister dove into her food. As she stuffed more cheese fries into her mouth, Levi pulled a ring box out of his jacket and gently placed it on the table.

Sister stared at the box first, then slowly reached for it. "What's this?"

"Take a look," Levi said.

Sister opened the ring box and found a folded piece of paper. Shaking her head, she looked at Levi and cracked up as she unfolded the paper and got a gander of what was on it: it was an ad for a stunning diamond ring he'd torn out of a magazine.

"One day, that's going to be yours," he said. "I promise."

Sister appreciated Levi's sincerity and was just about to tell him as much when clapping from a single pair of hands interrupted the quiet of their romantic moment. And when they turned toward the sound and their eyes settled on their excited audience, both Sister and Levi lost their breath as they realized just who was applauding Levi's efforts.

"Oh my God, it's . . ." Sister began as she adjusted her dress, patted her hair and pushed a wide grin across her face. Levi was shocked and pretty jazzed too. Standing right there over their table was Satin Struthers, the famous comedian, dressed in a fresh navy-blue pinstriped, tailorfitted suit. The reflection from his brilliant gold cuff links bounced off the metal napkin holder on the table. A Leica camera hung casually around his neck.

"Brother, that is some of the smoothest shit I've seen in a long time," said Satin, who was flanked by two beautiful women and his right-hand man, Ham. "You see this cat, Ham? What's your name, brother?"

"Levison. They call me Levi."

Satin smirked a bit. "Here I been buying these women the real deal when all I had to do is put a picture in a box," he said. "I'm 'bout to get me some scissors and some magazines and be like my boy Levi here," he added, turning his fingers into scissors. "Clip, clip, clip, hussies!"

Satin and his hangers-on laughed heartily, but Levi narrowed his eyes and bristled. Even their waiter, who was standing practically halfway across the room, could see how Levi's temples moved as he angrily ground his teeth. Sister was keen to Satin's insult, but it was Satin who held her attention.

"Can I see?" Satin asked, holding his hand out to Sister. He locked eyes with her, making clear that he was more interested in her than any stupid magazine photo, and she responded in kind, softening her gaze as she slowly handed him the paper. Levi shifted in his chair just a bit.

"That's nice, real nice," Satin said, barely looking at the picture as he smiled at Sister. "You got a good man here," he said, pressing the paper back into her hands. Then he focused his attention on Levi and went in for the kill: "I used to come here, too, when I was struggling back in the day," he said simply. "Good cheap food. Nice meeting you, Levi."

And with that, Satin walked on with his entourage, not even bothering to look back at the couple—dismissing them, their conversation, their moment. Levi was crushed.

"I better get you home," he said, tossing a few dollars onto the table and grabbing his hat off the back of the chair. He helped Sister into her coat and, without another word, headed to the door. Had he not been angry, had he not been trying to save face by leaving as quickly as possible, he would have noticed Sister turning back to give Satin a sly, mischievous smile—one that was met by the flash of Satin's camera. He wanted her, and right now, Satin was going to keep a piece of her in his shiny Leica.

Until they met again.

# CHAPTER 5

MISS WATERS WAITED for Emma to disappear behind the curtains in the back of the dress shop before she pulled the tattered photo album from the small shopping bag she carried into work each day. Not that she was trying to start any mess with Emma—Miss Waters knew she'd probably catch an attitude and a nasty talking-to for dredging up old memories of Emma's work as an entertainer. But lately, Sparkle had been slipping in a lot more questions about both her mother's days as a backup singer in Detroit and Harlem and the music she'd written for her own album, and Miss Waters figured if Emma wouldn't recount her star turn to her baby girl, she would. After all, nobody knew the story better than Sara Waters, her very best friend who was there before Emma got famous and there, too, when she'd hit rock bottom. And though Emma had tried to scrub away every memory of her life as a singer when she finally found her way out of the gutter and up to God, Miss Waters thought the pictures and stories and history and successes

59

of Emma's singing career important enough to hold on to. To cherish.

"Your mama doesn't know I saved this here photo album and she'll probably try to crucify me when she finds out I fished it out of the garbage can all those years ago, but I thought you should see it," Miss Waters said, pushing aside the fabric on the counter and gently placing the tattered book in front of Sparkle.

Sparkle lit up; she made quick work of diving into the album.

"Easy, now," Miss Waters warned. "The book is fragile."

"Oh, sorry," Sparkle said hesitantly as she gently pulled back the cover and leaned into the first of the pictures. There was her mother, young and lovely, in a beautiful sparkled gown with a lengthy slit, her eyes closed seemingly in ecstasy as she leaned into a microphone and sang her song. She looked sexy—the sexiest Sparkle had ever seen her mother, who, as the head seamstress in her own dressmaking shop and a child of the Lord, never wore a dress or skirt higher than the lowest section of her calf.

"She was so pretty," Sparkle sighed.

"Hard to believe it's the same woman, huh?" Miss Waters said, leaning into the photo album to take another look for herself.

"I mean, she's still pretty . . ." Sparkle countered quickly.

"No, she's not," Miss Waters snapped so loud Sparkle took her attention off the pictures and focused on her mother's best friend. "She's mad all the time. Can't be pretty and mad at the same time."

Sparkle wasn't going to touch that one. She refocused on the photo album, her eyes poring over the snapshots that had been carefully glued to the album's cardboard pages. After a few pages, her eyes settled on a picture of a handsome, dark-skinned man holding a trumpet. "Oh, there's Dee's daddy," she said, tapping her finger on the picture. Next to the photo was a small inscription handwritten in cursive: *Minton's Playhouse, 1945.*

Miss Waters looked at it for a moment and offered up a faint smile, then tapped her finger on a different picture, adjacent to the page they'd been perusing. "Here's a good one of yours and Sister's daddy," she said.

Sparkle leaned into the picture, taking in every inch of the man and her mother, who was hugging him. He looked smooth with his drumsticks in his hands; his mustache was pencil thin—as dark as the thick mane that was gelled to his head. His white tuxedo and bowtie washed him out, made him look like a white man. If she didn't have that special black-people sixth sense that spotted Negro blood in even the lightest and brightest of the bunch, she might have thought he was white. But that picture was from the early 1940s; there was no way her mother, unmistakably a Negro, would be hugging on a white man—even in the bowels of a progressive Harlem nightclub.

"Cute, but no good," Miss Waters said after the two stared at the picture for a few seconds more. Then, lifting Sparkle's chin, she added: "Got to watch out for those cute ones. They make a lot of promises."

Sparkle let her words settle a bit; instantly, she got a vision of Stix sweet-talking her and kissing her and then telling her he wanted a word with Sister. *Yes, the cute ones were good at making promises, weren't they*, she thought.

Mama's voice broke Sparkle's concentration and made both the women jump to attention. "Going to be the first store in Detroit to have these," she said, walking up with the top half of a black mannequin.

"She's pretty, Mama," Sparkle offered, shooting Miss Waters a look.

Miss Waters didn't bother trying to hide the book or pretend it wasn't there. She simply held it up and smiled a wicked grin. "Look what I found," she said, waving it in Emma's face. "The other, nicer you."

Emma snatched the album from Miss Waters's hands and slammed it shut. "Sparkle, go to lunch," she snapped. She tossed the album under the counter and didn't give it a second look. "And you," she said to Miss Waters, "come on so I can stretch some fabric across your ever-expanding behind."

Sparkle could see the anger on her mother's face. She didn't want to be anywhere near the dress shop while Mama gave her friend a piece of her mind about showing her old pictures and dragging up the past, and so she quickly grabbed her purse and headed for the door. Sparkle didn't know much about her mother's singing career, but of this much she was certain: Emma moved heaven and earth to keep her memories buried deep inside her, and anyone who dared shine a light on them had better be prepared for the wrath. Sparkle wanted no part of it.

And so she headed to the one place in Detroit that brought her joy: Juke's Record Store. It was just a few blocks from Mama's dress shop but felt like a whole new world

when Sparkle walked in; it was packed with dreamers and
music lovers and people her age who just wanted to hang
out, hear the latest hits and maybe take home a record and
a phone number or two. James Brown's "I Got That Feeling" was blasting when she flipped through the stacks of
records in search of new music to check out in her listening
booth. It was here where Sparkle discovered new songwriting techniques and arrangements—where she could get lost
in a good lyric and be inspired to think up a few new songs
of her own. On this particular afternoon, she was letting
the Rolling Stones, Percy Sledge and Sergio Mendes help
her escape her mother's anger, Stix's wishy-washy affection
and persistence, Sister's depression—all of it.

Mick Jagger was screaming about cross-fire hurricanes
and driving rain when a tap against her listening-booth
window interrupted her escape. Startled, Sparkle looked
up to find Stix, flashing a smile and waving like he'd just
found a long-lost buddy. Part of Sparkle was happy to see
him—his face, his smile—they never got tired. But a bigger
part of her was still mad at him for playing her—for using
her to get to Sister. Sparkle hadn't talked to him since that
fateful Sunday when he crashed the choir dressing room
and, rather than hug Sparkle, ask her how she was doing
or offer to take her out on a proper date, he made a beeline
for Sister and went to work trying to woo her into being
the lead singer of a girl group that would sing all her music
and relegate her to the background. And now, here he was,
smiling and waving and acting like nothing was wrong.

*Jerk.*

Sparkle returned to reading the record cover of the

Percy Sledge LP without smiling or waving back at Stix. Undeterred, Stix tried to open the booth, but Sparkle already had locked it, so he was left to state his case through the glass. With a store full of people watching him beg.

"Come on," he pleaded. "Talk to me."

Sparkle gave him nothing.

"I got Cliff Bell's!" he yelled, thinking that would snap her out of whatever funk she was in.

He was right—it did get her attention. But not in the way he'd hoped. Sparkle rushed out of the listening booth and straight out of the record store, with Stix hot on her heels. By the time he caught up to her, she was unwrapping a sandwich and shoving it down her throat.

"What are you doing?" he asked.

Sparkle took another bite. "I only get an hour for lunch," she said, bread flying out of her mouth.

"Sparkle, I know I hurt your feelings. And I'm sorry. But I'm only trying to do what's best for us," he said, grabbing the remaining half of Sparkle's sandwich. "And hopefully, you'll be performing in a few nights, so you won't be needing the other half of this."

Sparkle reeled back from the insult. "So now I'm fat?" she snapped. "You really have a way with words," she said, snatching her sandwich back from Stix and stomping back down the street toward her mother's shop.

Stix loved her spirit, but he was starting to feel like he'd blown his one shot at managing the one group he knew would hit. "I signed you up for this Thursday night," he called after Sparkle. "Eight o'clock. I'll be waiting!" And then, to himself, he added: "Hope you make it."

Defeated, Stix headed back in the store to a listening booth of his own. But rather than play a record, he sat in silence and, for the first time in a long time, sent up a prayer that Sparkle not only heard what he had to say, but would come to her senses and show up to Cliff Bell's on Thursday, ready to make everybody a star.

Sparkle hummed as she scribbled the words *nothing's wrong, it's all right, my man* into her journal. Dolores had her sister's head bent at an almost impossible angle as she ran a hot comb through the hair at the nape of Sparkle's neck, but Sparkle didn't want to stop writing—this song had a hold on her and she needed to get the words down while the melody was still fresh.

"That sounds real nice, Sparkle," Dolores said as she gently parted and greased Sparkle's hair and readied the hot comb for another run through her curls. "What's the name of that one?"

"I think I'm going to call it 'Giving Him Something He Can Feel,'" Sparkle said.

"Well, all right now," Dolores grinned. "And who's that one for . . ."

Before Dolores could escalate her teasing, Sister marched in to Sparkle's room, waving an envelope. "I got my first check," she said, tossing her purse on the dresser.

"Let me see," Sparkle said, snatching the envelope from her sister's hands. She took a peek. "Ninety-six dollars?" she screamed. "For two weeks of standing on your feet, kissing rich white women's butts?"

Sister collapsed on Sparkle's bed, exasperated. "I'm never going to get out of here," she sighed.

Sparkle looked at her hopeless sister, then tossed a mischievous look in Dolores's direction. Dolores quietly egged her on. "Tell her," she mouthed to Sparkle.

Sparkle closed her journal and cleared her throat. "Stix said we could make anywhere from five hundred to a thousand dollars a night if we won Cliff Bell's talent contest," she shot out.

"Don't say it all dry like that," Dolores demanded. "Sell it!"

"Oh, so y'all talking to Stix now?" Sister asked, staring at Sparkle.

"No, *she's* talking to Stix," Dolores shot out. "I was talking to her and now we're talking to you."

Truth is, Sparkle didn't want to talk to Stix after she left him standing in the middle of the street, but she was no dummy: she knew winning Cliff Bell's was a big deal for anyone who wanted to be bigger than a talent-show artist in Detroit. And if you were making it in Detroit, you were destined to make it big everywhere, because Motown was where stars were made. So she'd marched herself over to the club and talked her way into the lounge area, where the manager was prepping his crew for the evening's opening. He refused to talk to Sparkle, but she did manage to smile really pretty and make nice talk with one of the security guys, who didn't mind answering her questions—namely, what could a pretty girl like her with two beautiful sisters win if they lit up the stage and brought the Cliff Bell's crowd to its feet? "It's not just what you win that night, pretty girl," the bouncer said. "You win Cliff Bell's, you own this town. You're making five hundred, a thousand dollars a night at some of the better clubs around."

"A thousand?" Sparkle said, her eyes widening. "A night?"

"Yup. And if you and your sisters are anywhere near as good as you claim and you start bringing home all that cash, maybe you can remember ol' Buster and stop by Cliff Bell's and buy me a drink," the bouncer added.

"I just might do that," Sparkle said, rushing out of the lounge.

And though her brain was telling her to leave him alone, her heart and her legs had another thing in mind for Jeremiah "Stix" Warren. Both led her back to the record store, where she marched right up to the listening booth where Stix was, barged in, kissed him on the lips and told him he'd better be ready because come Thursday, she and her sisters were going to tear down the house at Cliff Bell's.

"Are you serious?" Stix said, jumping up to hug Sparkle. "You're good with the arrangement and everything?"

"I'm good," Sparkle said.

"What about your sister?" Stix said, pulling Sparkle closer to him. "Is she good?"

"Let me worry about her," she said. "Trust me. I got it."

And she did. There just weren't a whole lot of people that Sister listened to. In fact, there was only one person who even remotely could convince her to do anything— and that person was Sparkle.

"You know what they say about falling in love with the

person you work for, right?" Sister said to Sparkle. "You shouldn't eat where you . . ."

"It's the other way around," Dolores said.

"She gets my point," Sister snapped.

"I thought about it," Sparkle interrupted. "I want to do this for me. Not him."

Sister took a beat to think about it. "So how much can we make a week?" she asked, her question punctuated by a huge smile.

"Yes!" Sparkle said excitedly, moving so suddenly that Dolores burned her ear with the hot comb. "Ow! Thank you," she said sarcastically to her sister.

"That's all well and good, but how are all of us at the same time going to get past Mama for at least three hours?" Sister asked.

Sister was the master of the worst-case scenarios and of the three sisters, Sparkle was the scaredy-cat of them all. But Dolores was the quick one of the bunch. From the moment Stix came to the choir dressing room to pitch their girl group, Dolores started hatching their escape plan. She'd run it over and over again in her mind—maybe they could sneak out one at a time? Maybe the three of them could claim they were doing an all-night "shut-in" for teenagers at one of the choir members' houses? Maybe they could find a way to get Mama out of the house while they performed.

Yeah, right.

Dolores knew full well that no matter what they conjured up, there was no way they were going to fool Emma Anderson into letting her daughters stay out for hours on a Thursday night—and if she even suspected the three of them were plotting to start a singing group and perform in a nightclub, she'd bring serious bodily harm to each of them. And so Dolores conjured up the only plan she could think of that would ensure they could do Cliff Bell's without Mama killing them.

"Let me worry about that," she said to Sister and Sparkle after they officially formed their group. "Sparkle, you just make sure we have a good song. Sister, you make sure we look nice and have some good moves. I'll handle Mama."

Come that Thursday night, Dolores "handled" Mama all right.

After hurrying into their performance dresses and fussing over their makeup and hair, there the three of them were on the night of their big performance, standing over their mother, who was sleeping soundly on the couch. Almost too soundly.

"How much did you give her?" Sparkle asked Dolores, leaning in to make sure their mother was still breathing.

"Look, I know me and Mama don't get along," Sister chimed in. "But did you kill her?"

To be honest, Dolores wasn't sure if the drug she'd slipped into Mama's tea would mean the end of her. The guy she got the tiny packet from was a med student and he'd assured her that it would knock her mother out for a few hours with very few side effects—maybe a headache in the morning, but nothing more serious than that. Dolores used exactly the amount he told her to add to Mama's tea, and after a little coaxing from her daughter, Mama drank it all down and passed out on the couch, just like her friend said she would, so Dolores had to trust that she would wake up, too.

"I'm darn near a doctor," she insisted, but only half-heartedly. "I did it right. She's fine. But let's get going. It's supposed to wear off in three hours."

"Oh God, help us," Sparkle said, taking one last look at her mother as Sister and Dolores grabbed her hands and ran for the door.

Levi was leaning against Mama's car, waiting for the sisters when they got outside. He smiled big when he saw Sister; she gave him a coy grin when her eyes met with his. Hastily, they climbed into the car, taking one nervous last look to make sure none of the neighbors were watching them commit grand theft larceny. It was 8 PM, though; men had come home from work, dutiful wives had already served dinner, cleaned the kitchen and put the kids to bed, and only people who were up to no good were on the street at that time of night on a Thursday, so really, they were safe. And when the girls piled in and Levi put Mama's car in neutral and let it roll out of the driveway, and then started the car and pulled away from the house, all four of them knew that at that moment, in that space and time, they were moving toward something phenomenal.

Something that would change each of their lives forever.

Fifteen minutes later, Stix and half of black Detroit were out in front of Cliff Bell's, one of the most famous clubs among the lounges, restaurants, pubs and burlesques dotting Detroit's Park Avenue. The signature club, opened in 1935 to tons of press for its luxurious mahogany and brass art-deco interior, had been a must-play spot on the jazz club circuit, drawing the likes of such heavyweights as Dizzy Gillespie, Louis Armstrong, Ella Fitzgerald and countless others while it was a whites-only club, but when Motown took over the music charts and the club's owners recognized the financial benefits of catering to a Negro clientele in a city full of Negroes, black acts who found success on the pop and R&B charts were regularly invited to the stage to entertain Cliff Bell's patrons. Later, when its owners recognized Detroit was the mecca of new artists and music, it began to open its stage up to amateurs at its popular Thursday-night talent show, making the Cliff Bell's Talent Search one of the must-win talent shows for anybody who was making a serious run at becoming a star. You win Cliff Bell's, you win the entertainment game—at least in Detroit. And winning in Detroit mattered.

Stix, who'd arrived at the club an hour early to survey the stage, work the crowd and have himself a drink to calm his nerves, checked his watch: it was 8:30 and there still was no sign of the girls. When he looked up, though, there she was—Sparkle, with her sisters and Levi in tow. She looked so beautiful, he could hardly contain his smile. Neither could Sparkle.

"Surprised?" she asked.

"Not at all," Stix said, lying. Though she'd said she would convince Sister to sing with them, Stix hadn't heard from Sparkle after the moment they shared in the record store, and he knew that if he reached out and pushed for Sister any more than he already had, he would likely drive her away. So he kept quiet, and trusted his silence would swing her his way. Thank God, it did.

Stix followed the group into Cliff Bell's and said a silent "thank you" to Him.

Sparkle was too excited to pray. She was blown away by the beauty of the club and the energy in the room—the sound bouncing off the walls and enthusiasm of the crowd. This space, this moment—this was where she was meant to be. She was sure of it. Until, that is, her eyes trained on the stage, where another girl group was performing—much to the delight of their rapt audience. They were good. Really good.

"We come a dime a dozen, don't we?" Sister said, focusing on the group at exactly the same time as Sparkle.

Stix, nervous that Sister was right, kept it positive. "I'm going to get the girls signed in and backstage," he said simply to Levi as he took one last look at the women onstage and then signaled Sparkle, Sister and Dolores to the rear.

"Go get 'em, baby," Levi said enthusiastically, completely missing the worry pervading Sister and her sisters.

Levi hung back and soaked up the scene, feeling a lot like he'd finally arrived. There he was in Cliff Bell's with the finest woman in the room about to take over the stage. He couldn't afford to buy her a meal there, or even dessert and a cocktail without putting a hurting on his wallet, but that didn't stop him from feeling like he was a boss. Levi's mood was quickly deflated, though, when Satin, with that ever-present camera hanging around his neck and a couple of fine women and his sidekick, Ham, by his side, noticed him and walked over.

"You're Picture-in-a-Box brother, right? I don't forget a face," Satin said, snapping his fingers and pointing a finger right at Levi's eyes. "I'll forget your name in a minute . . ."

"It's Levi," said Levi, annoyed.

"Fellas," Satin said, turning to his friends, "this is . . . see, I forgot already." His cronies laughed like that was the funniest joke they'd ever heard.

"You need to add that into your act," Ham said, mid-chuckle. "That was good." Noticing Levi wasn't amused, he added: "Lighten up—they're just jokes."

Levi hesitated for a moment and then finally laughed along. It was certainly better, he calculated, than standing there getting sore about it. Just a few seconds ago, he was The Man. He wasn't planning on letting anyone, even Satin, steal that joy.

Just then, Stix walked up. "They're all set," he said.

"I'd like you to meet Satin Struthers," Levi told Stix, tossing his chin in Satin's direction.

Stix, oblivious to the mini-drama that had just un-folded, pumped Satin's hand. "You're a funny man," he said, smiling cheerfully.

"Thank you," Satin said.

"This is my cousin," Levi continued, finding his voice. "He manages my girlfriend and her sisters. They're per-forming tonight."

"I hope they're good," Satin said. "I'm looking for a group to open up my next show."

Stix's mind went into overdrive on that one. First Cliff Bell's, then the opening act on Satin Struthers's comedy tours? That was big time; the girls would get a ridiculous amount of exposure hanging with Satin, who'd broken bar-riers to become one of the most popular and well-respected black comedians among white audiences. Being his open-ing act meant an automatic entrée to the very producers, directors and show hosts who'd opened their doors to the likes of Aretha Franklin, Diana Ross and the Supremes, Stevie Wonder and the Jackson 5. Stix could hardly contain his excitement. It was on.

As Stix let his dreams get ahead of him, the club owner, Mr. Bell, walked up to Satin and offered his hand. "Satin, it's a pleasure to see you again," he said. "We have a nice table for you up front."

"Come with us," Satin said over his shoulder. Levi and Stix didn't hesitate; they followed right behind Satin, pleased to join the famous comedian in prime house seats. But before Levi could catch a good stride, Satin struck again. "I only have one extra seat," he said slyly. "It's probably best I talk to the manager than the boyfriend."

Stix didn't hesitate—just kept on walking with Satin and his entourage while Levi stood back and seethed. Satin had won, twice, and he was beside himself with anger— so much so that he practically blacked out as the crowd cheered the group that was onstage, getting the crowd so hyped, half of them had risen to their feet to rock to its song.

Levi may not have noticed how well the group was doing, but Sister sure did. The girls had the crowd captivated, and the lead singer was using all of her womanly ways to work over the audience. By the time she'd finished shimmying across the stage and she and her backup singers had taken a bow, the entire crowd delivered to them a roaring applause—helped along by Buddy, the master of ceremonies, who stepped to the stage with a huge grin and some encouraging words for the ladies. Well, if you could call it that.

"Whoa, they were amazing. It's my birthday tonight and I'm going to wish for that thick one's attention and a quick divorce," Buddy exclaimed, the crowd returning his enthusiasm with roaring laughter. "Oh hey," he continued, "I see we have Mr. Satin Struthers in the audience tonight!"

Every neck in the club stretched to get a look at Satin—much to Satin's pleasure. And Stix's, too. He was quite pleased to be up in the mix, for sure. To mark the moment for posterity, Satin lifted his camera and took a picture of Buddy.

"Coming next to the stage is another girl group," Buddy said. "Everybody wants to be The Supremes. Well, let's see if this group of sisters can give Diana and the other two a run for their money."

That was their cue: in the wings, Sparkle and Dolores nervously removed their coats, scared of what was to come but determined to take the stage and be more than "just another girl group." They were shaken, though, when the rival group walked past them, got a gander of their dresses and guffawed all the way back to the dressing area.

Sparkle looked nervously at Dolores and Dolores returned the gaze. They did look a little "church girly" in the sweet church dresses their mother had hand-sewn for them this past Easter. They were the finest dresses the girls owned—navy-blue affairs with three-quarter sleeves, button-down sweetheart collars and a belted waist that blossomed into at least a yard of fabric that floated almost down to their ankles. When they wore them to church, everyone raved, which was why Dolores and Sparkle thought it was a good idea to wear them for their big Cliff Bell's debut.

They had no time to encourage each other on their outfits, though; instead, they focused on Sister, who was pulling a pair of high-heeled shoes out of her purse. Dee noticed first, and nudged Sparkle to take a gander at what was peeking from behind Sister's coat. And when Sister dropped that coat to reveal a slinky dress she'd clearly gotten when she was in New York, Sparkle and Dolores lost it.

"What the hell is that?" Dolores demanded.

"You want to win this money, don't you?" Sister said nonchalantly, running her hands down the sides of her hips to smooth out the wrinkles.

Onstage, Buddy introduced the group: "Please welcome, Sister and Her Sisters!"

"Showtime," Sister said. "Now go on out there and sing the hook a couple times."

"What? Sister, this ain't what we rehearsed," said an incredulous Sparkle, who'd written and arranged the song and, more importantly, rehearsed it with her sisters practically every free second they had over the past few days. Changing up the routine seconds before they were about to take the stage was *not* an option—at least not in Sparkle's mind.

"I know what I'm doing," Sister insisted. "Just go," she said, pushing Sparkle and Dolores onto the stage as the band began playing the intro to Sparkle's song, "Hooked on Your Love." With no other choice but to do as Sister said, Sparkle and Dolores took their places at their mics and swayed back and forth and did as they were told. "What can I do? With this feeling? Hooked on your love, sweet love, love," they sang nervously.

The crowd, clearly unimpressed, began to heckle them.

"Where'd y'all get them dresses? This ain't Sunday school!" someone yelled, cracking up the crowd.

The girls pressed on, but panic began to seep in. Stix, seeing Satin chuckle at the joke, dropped his head into his hands. His big shot—gone.

"Get this man a drink!" Satin yelled out. "He's gonna need it to get through this."

Sister looked on at the impending disaster but waited one more beat before she made her entrance. She spotted Satin in the audience and smiled.

Showtime.

Sister slinked onto the stage like honey in hot tea—making all space and time stand still. And when she stepped to the mic, the sound from her mouth floated into the air and dropped on the crowd like a thousand feathers on bare skin. Everyone in the room was absolutely mesmerized.

Stix recognized the song as the one Sparkle had sung for him back at her house, but under Sister's care, it was raw and sexy. Delicious. And the crowd loved it. Sparkle and Dolores did, too. And wherever their sister led them, they followed—getting off on the effect the three of them were having on the crowd. Sister seduced the men into wanting her and women into wanting to be her. And when her eyes fell on Satin and Levi, she toyed with the two, looking them directly in the eyes and singing straight down into their souls. "I like the way we carry on/Hope you understand my feelings/Got me just a reeling," she sang while staring at Satin. He lifted his camera to take a photo, but was too intrigued by Sister to click the shutter. He was hooked. In fact, the entire club was hooked—so into the song that they'd already memorized the words and sang the chorus along with the women. Stix sang the loudest.

Levi? He just slunk against the wall, nursing his drink and his hurt feelings. He was so upset that he didn't bother making his way backstage to congratulate Sister, as he'd promised. Instead, he hid in the shadows of that wall, mean-mugging Satin and his crew through the rest of the talent show, taking his eyes off them only when Buddy came back onstage to announce the winner.

"It was a long night and there was a lot of good talent on the stage of the world-famous Cliff Bell's," Buddy said. "But there can be only one winner. And the winner of Cliff Bell's talent contest is . . ."

Sparkle, in the wings, and Stix, sitting at Satin's table with his hands clenched, both looked like they were going to faint—as if the moments between the word *is* and the name of the winner was sucking away every breath of air on which their bodies could subsist.

Buddy put them out of their misery and announced the winner: "Sister and Her Sisters!"

Shocked, excited, insanely happy, the sisters embraced as Stix made his way to the stage to congratulate them. "You were right," Sparkle laughed into Stix's ear as he folded her into a tight embrace. "Sister is amazing. I could never do that!"

And, with everyone watching and without a care in the world, the two kissed—right there on the stage, as every-one celebrated around them. Whatever Stix wanted, Sparkle was ready to give it to him.

On their celebratory ride back home, Stix made clear he had demands. Like a coach, he excitedly called out from the backseat what the girls needed to do to continue on their bid to take over the music world. "This was nothing!" he shouted. "I'm telling you, I can have you booked all over this city. Diana better watch out. Sister, you were amazing. Amazing!"

Sister smiled confidently, holding on to Levi's arm as he steered Emma's car through the streets of Detroit.

"Sparkle! We need more of your songs. The kind we talked about," Stix continued.

"Okay," she said excitedly.

"We need something hot. Something to make the people pay to see us. Can you do that?" Stix asked.

"I can do that," she said.

"We need . . ."

"We need some new dresses, Mr. Manager," Sister interrupted.

"We need to get home before Mama wakes up," Dolores said, bringing everyone in the car back down to reality. "I'm not trying to die."

Stix tapped Levi's shoulder. "Levi, be careful driving. You have my future in this car."

Sparkle beamed at Stix and then turned to the window, watching the city lights blur into each other.

They were on their way.

# CHAPTER 6

Stix stood out front of the Sugar Shack in the rain, pulling his jacket collar tightly around his neck as he stared through the tiny window on the metal door. It was a gruff, dusty pool hall just down the street from Levi's place in Twelfth Street—a place where characters both normal and notorious whiled away their time, always with a cold beer, a cigarette and some dice or a pool stick in their hands. Levi had spent plenty of time there, rolling dice and talking smack whenever his paycheck didn't stretch and he needed to dredge up an extra buck or two for the rent. And when Stix made clear that he needed some fast cash to outfit Sister and Her Sisters, Levi pointed his little cousin in the direction of the Sugar Shack, where he knew Stix could put his pool skills to real good use. It was Levi who'd taught him that particular skill—the art of the pool hall hustle. Back in Kansas City, when he moved out of his mother's place and tried to make it on his own while he hustled as a manager for a few small, local jazz artists, it was a skill that came in real handy, too. No one saw Stix coming for them; his baby face—even at age nineteen, he looked no older than fourteen—got his opponent every time, and made it particularly easy to take home enough cash to drop off a few dollars at his mother's house, hit Levi off with a little something toward the rent and pay for minor expenses incurred by the two artists—a drummer and a trumpeter—on his roster.

Now, his new babies needed new dresses and shoes, and Stix was on a mission to get them, by any means necessary. Plus, he needed to make himself scarce for a few hours while Sister and Levi had some private time at Levi's place, where Stix had been crashing on the couch while he tried to get his music management company off the ground. Damn if he was going to get in the way of young love—or make Sister's Happy Train run off course. She liked Levi. Levi was crazy about her. And as long as Sister was happy, everybody was happy—and eating.

Stix cracked his neck and zoned in on a pool hustler he knew he could pick off easily for a few dollars. He had a big mouth, that guy, and some money in his pocket, but he wasn't nearly as good as he thought he was, Stix quickly surmised. Stix wanted all his money.

Stix entered the Sugar Shack and walked directly over to the bar. After the bartender gave him his beer, he stood by the pool table closest to the window and quietly watched the game. When it was over and the big-mouthed guy loudly collected his winnings and ordered another round, Stix quietly said, "I got next."

"Oh, young buck—you don't want none of this," the big-mouthed guy said as he counted his cash—by the looks of it, about $300. Enough for three pretty new dresses, three pairs of shoes and a wig for Dolores.

Stix pulled five crisp twenty-dollar bills out of his pocket and gently laid them on the table. "Round them up," he said simply.

Big Mouth couldn't refuse.

What he didn't realize, but learned pretty quickly, was that the quiet guy with the twenties had a bigger mouth and a better game than he did. All day.

"Daddy don't need a new pair of shoes—got those!" Stix yelled as he stalked a circle around the pool table, chalking up his pool stick and staring down the six ball. "Daddy need three new pretty dresses. Six ball, corner pocket."

His shot crackled like thunder. As did his cackle when the ball raced into the hole, behind all the others he'd expertly shot without giving Big Mouth so much as one turn at the table.

Stix kept talking smack. "I want to thank you for your involuntary contribution to the Stix Incorporated wardrobe fund," he said, sinking the eight ball. He smiled coyly at his opponent. "You were impressed with my big words, weren't you?" Stix added as he scooped up the wad of cash laid out on a nearby table. His opponent threw down his cue, picked up his hat and stomped out the door, just as Stix's next victim made it into the pool hall.

"Who got next?" Stix called out.

The new guy, this one bigger than the last, didn't say a word—just laid his $200 on the table.

"Well, all right—a man of few words," Stix smiled. "And soon to be of fewer dollars. I'll rack them, you break."

Within ten minutes, Stix was again running game. "Eight ball, side pocket. Enough said!" He sunk it and grabbed the money off the table—$300 extra in his pocket in just under an hour. "Yeah," he said, counting the cash to make sure it was all there.

But this opponent wasn't going to go down so easy. He swung on Stix with a heavy sledgehammer of an arm. But Stix was too quick for him. Besides teaching him how to play the game, Levi had taught Stix how to handle sore losers. With just three punches, Stix deftly whipped the man's ass and was about to give him a few extra licks for swinging on him when a gunshot rang out. Stix and the sore loser froze.

"Y'all know I don't allow this kind of mess in my place," said Sugar, the woman who owned the pool hall. "Stix, get yo' narrow ass on out of here. And Lee Junior, stop wanting to fight every time you lose."

Stix didn't hesitate to get going. He had some dresses to buy.

Sparkle and Dolores were waiting for him when he arrived at Ms. Peach's Boutique, a small dress shop on the south side. Ms. Peach was one of Emma's chief rivals. And the last thing the girls needed to do was be seen squeezing into Peach's fancy dresses, but she was the best in town and, unlike Mama, didn't specialize in the church wear that would get Sister and Her Sisters booed off the stage. So Stix insisted on buying their outfits there. Sparkle and Dolores, who'd skipped out of work and school to meet

Stix, dragged Tune Ann along so that she could go into the boutique, take a look at what Peach had stocked, then describe each of the dresses to them so that they could figure out which to buy without having to go in.

Both of them nearly jumped out of their skin when Stix walked up and tapped them on their shoulders.

"Stix, geez, you scared me!" Sparkle said, clutching her heart.

"What are you two doing lurking around Peach's like you're about to steal something?" he asked, giving Sparkle and Dolores warm hugs as he questioned them.

"Tune Ann is inside picking out our dresses. You know we can't go in there," Dolores said.

"Wait—Tune Ann?" Stix said incredulously. "You sent your best church girlfriend to pick out dresses for you?"

"Well, you know we can't go in there, Stix," Sparkle said.

"Look," Stix insisted, "leave the costuming to me. I think your man knows better what would look sexy on you, Dolores and Sister than your badly dressed, non-singing, totally not sexy friend."

Sparkle giggled. "Leave Tune Ann alone," she said.

"Yeah, yeah," Dolores interrupted. "You got the money, Stix? Because no matter how good your taste in dresses, you need to have the cash to get them 'cause we sure don't have it."

Stix pulled the wad of pool winnings out of his pocket. "I told you, I got the outfits covered. The question is, have you all been practicing? Because you did really good at Cliff Bell's, but if you want to be the best, you're going to have to really bring it when you get back up on that stage from now on."

"Oh, you don't have to worry about us," Sparkle said. "We're getting our job done."

And they were. From the moment the sisters took home first prize at the most important talent show in Detroit and Stix talked Mr. Bell into giving the group a regular feature before the Saturday-night sets, Sparkle, Dolores and Sister hit practice like it was their day jobs. Whenever Mama turned her back, went to sleep, left for Bible study or helped with the numerous tasks at her shop and at church, they were in the piano room, practicing their harmonies, learning Sparkle's new songs and making up dance routines to go with the new numbers they were debuting at Cliff Bell's. They even practiced a few times at Levi and Stix's place, testing out their moves to make sure they were sexy enough to get and keep the audience's attention.

And with every rehearsal, new song and performance, Sister and Her Sisters got better, more polished and so popular that within two months' time, they were drawing in standing-room-only crowds three nights a week at the club and making quite a name for themselves in Detroit.

Everybody loved Sister and Her Sisters—couldn't wait to see what they were wearing, what song they were singing, what provocative move Sister would make to get the whole club to perspire. In their latest song, "Jump," the whole crowd would go mad when Sister shimmied to the foot of the stage and purred, "You're doing fine/And now you're right on time/Have a ball/I hope my mama don't call."

Levi especially loved it; he helped Sister come up with that move. And he promised her that if she stared at him while she did it at their next show, he'd have something really special for her afterward. He craved her attention. What man wouldn't?

"Tonight was the best I've ever seen you," Levi said, rushing into the dressing room with a bouquet of flowers for Sister, who'd just given him a preview onstage of what he had coming the next time they were alone. "All of you," Levi added when he finally remembered that Sparkle and Dolores were part of the act, too. "But you," he said, turning his attention back to Sister, "were amazing."

Levi leaned in to kiss Sister, but she pulled back coyly. "You'll mess up my lipstick," she said, smiling, taking the flowers from his hands and smelling them.

"As much as I would love to mess it up, I have to get to work," Levi said, still staring hungrily at Sister.

"Since when did you have a graveyard shift?" Stix inquired.

"Well, Cuz, since I got a woman that needs things," Levi said, winking at Sister.

Sister returned his smile as Levi made his way to the dressing-room door. When he opened it, he found Satin there, about to knock.

"Satin," Stix called out. "I didn't know you were in the house tonight. Sparkle, Dolores, this is Satin Struthers."

"Pleased to meet you," said Satin.

"Pleased to meet you," Sparkle said, trying to contain her excitement over meeting the famous comedian she'd seen in the crowd and in comedy shows on television but had never personally met. He was the first star she'd seen up close.

Dolores wasn't impressed. "Hi," she barely managed.

"And this is . . ." Stix said, turning to Sister.

Sister cut him off. "We know each other," she smiled, looking at Satin flirtatiously. He returned the favor—much to Levi's chagrin.

"First, I want to say I enjoyed your performance," Satin continued, focusing solely on Sister.

"Thank you," Sister said, fluffing her hair. Her words were short, but she was long on body language. It was speaking to Satin—calling him, enticing him. And with every batted eyelash, every slight hand movement and hip caress, Levi grew more angry.

"And secondly," Satin continued, "I wanted to give you this."

He handed Sister a jewelry box. She was so excited that she unconsciously tossed her flowers back to Levi so that she could take the small, black box into her beautifully manicured hands.

"Wait a minute, brother . . ." Levi started. But his protestation was met with Sister's shriek.

"Oh my God!" she exclaimed as she stared into the jewelry box. In it was a huge diamond ring set on a gold band, with smaller baguettes lining either side. Levi wasn't sure, but it looked just like the ring he'd shown Sister a picture of. Maybe even a better one. Defeated, he looked at his flowers and dropped them to his side.

A coy grin washed over Satin's face. "Some friends of mine are having a party tonight," he continued. "Thought you might like to go along with me. We could celebrate your success and get better acquainted." Then, finally realizing he and Sister were not the only ones in the room, he focused on Dolores and Sparkle. "Of course, that invitation extends to all of you."

"Levi's on his way to work and my sisters have to get home," Sister said quickly—her words making everybody in the room uncomfortable. Everybody, that is, except her and Satin.

"I'll wait for you outside," Satin said, giving her one last smile. He looked Levi up and down from his Afro to his high waters and slightly run-over shoes, adjusted his tailored suit jacket and opened the dressing-room door with a smirk on his face.

Levi, unable to take the slight, jumped on Satin and, in his struggle, smacked him, mussing his slicked hair.

"Somebody better get this mother . . ." Satin started as Stix pulled Levi off him. "Have you lost your mind? It takes ten minutes to get this hair in place." Satin patted his hair and ran his fingers across his mustache. "But that's okay. It was going to get messed up tonight anyway."

Levi rushed Satin again, but this time, Satin smacked the taste out of his mouth and gave Levi an icy stare that sent shivers down the spine of everyone standing in the room. "Don't you ever," Satin said sinisterly.

Before Levi could rush Satin a third time, Stix pushed him into the hallway, an act that may have saved Levi's life. Levi shook Stix off of him and straightened his jacket. "I'm tired of being broke! I work seven days a week, and for what?"

"She ain't worth it, man, let her go," Stix insisted, trying to calm Levi and using his body to separate him from the dressing room.

A beat later, Satin walked right past them, patting down his hair. "Got to have her to let her go," he said smoothly. "Semantics, brother. Semantics."

Satin laughed as Stix held Levi back. "She ain't worth it, man," Stix insisted, struggling to keep Levi away from Satin as he turned the corner and walked back out to the club.

Levi shook himself loose of Stix's grip. "If for no other reason than the drool you deposit on my couch every night, you should've had my back in there!" he yelled.

"I did!" Stix insisted.

"No," Levi countered. "You didn't."

"Man, this was business," Stix snapped. "Nothing personal."

Levi stared at his cousin; Stix's words stung more than Satin's slap. "You're right," he said, finally. "Nothing personal."

Levi slammed the bouquet of flowers into the dressing-room door and stalked out of the club and into the cool nighttime air, leaving Stix to ponder what he'd just done. From the moment the words formed on his lips, Stix knew he'd messed up—knew that he'd betrayed the one person in his life who'd always had his back. When Stix needed a place to escape to after leaving his mother's house, Levi didn't hesitate to make a paddle for him on the floor of his basement studio apartment in Kansas City—didn't hesitate to make sure that his little cousin had at least one hot meal in his belly and a way to make a little pocket change for all those big dreams he talked about during every waking hour. It was Levi, too, who didn't hesitate to move to Detroit with him, agreeing to be his wingman, confidant and provider as Stix slowly hustled his way into the entertainment business. Whatever he needed, Levi found a way to make sure he got it, sometimes even going without for himself. All because he wanted nothing more than to see his cousin make it. All because he *knew* his cousin could make it. And *that* was personal.

Stix slammed his hand against the wall and screamed out in frustration—mad that in that split second, he'd yielded to his tragic flaw: following his passion, everything—and everybody—else be damned.

Back in the dressing room, Sparkle jumped when she heard Stix holler. Pissed, she turned to Sister. "How could you do that to Levi?" she asked, incredulous.

Sister blew her off. "Levi's a grown man," she said, staring down at the diamond ring she'd slipped on her finger. "He didn't say nothing, why should I?"

"Don't listen to her," Dolores snapped at Sparkle. "She's darn near thirty and not married."

"Shut up," Sister snapped, priming herself for yet another Dolores/Sister verbal smackdown.

"But Levi loves you," Sparkle said, ignoring her sisters' bickering.

Sister finally took her focus off the ring and stared Sparkle in the face. "Spark," she said, taking her chin into her hand, "when you see a train that's finally going to get you where you're trying to go, you can't wait to live. You have to jump on it."

Sister pushed her way past Dolores and looked into the huge dressing-room mirror anchored on the vanity. She picked up a tube of lipstick and swiped it across her ruby-red lips, then applied mascara to her eyelashes and a little extra rouge to her cheeks. She stared into the mirror for a few seconds longer, as if having a conversation with herself. As if no one else was standing in the room watching her. And then she took one last look at her ring, grabbed her purse and walked out the door.

She never looked back.

# CHAPTER 7

Some things most everybody knew about Reverend Bryce: he was from Mississippi, down in those backwoods where they ran moonshine and found their fun in hideaway speakeasys and sometimes saw black bodies swinging from the giant oaks that stretched across the landscape of the Jim Crow South. He came to Detroit in search of money and respect as a small-time gangster and found Jesus down the barrel of a .45 pistol. And when he'd finally gotten himself together and let go of his attempts at being a big-city criminal, he realized that there was much more money to be had leading one of the biggest, best-attended churches in Detroit than there was running the streets, breaking the law and dodging bullets. Reverend Bryce still had some gangster ways about him, though. For example, he was expert at conning the women in his congregation into doing all the heavy lifting at his church—Emma included. He knew just the right combination of words and Bible verses to get the collection plates overflowing. And there wasn't a table in town that the widowed reverend hadn't planted his feet under for a free meal all seven days of the week.

And on this particular Sunday, it was Emma's turn to fill the pastor's belly—a duty she treasured almost as much as she did her love of the Lord. She'd gotten up early Sunday morning and put her pot roast in the oven, prepared her macaroni and cheese—the one with the roux and the three different cheeses that made it all fluffy and tangy— and got her collards going, all before it was time to leave for Sunday school. And when church was over, Emma ran out of the service before anyone could have a word with her, just so that she could make it back to the house to fry her chicken, mix up her special sherbert punch and ice the coconut cake she'd whipped up for dessert. Reverend was special to her. She wasn't going to miss the opportunity to impress.

Her daughters weren't nearly as impressed with the Reverend or his ways. But they tolerated him because, well, he was the pastor and they had to, at the very least, respect him. Even when he made a point of sitting at the end of the dinner table with the best view of the TV and watched shows while the women cooked, set the table and basically catered to his every whim.

"You sang lovely today, Sparkle," Reverend Bryce said as Sparkle set down his place setting. "It's like you were singing with a brand-new voice."

"Thank you, Reverend Bryce," Sparkle said, unsure where he was going with the compliment. He'd never noticed her singing before. And certainly never complimented her. Those compliments were reserved for Sister.

"But if you don't mind my asking, how can you hear me? I've never had a solo."

"You can always hear one of God's angels sing," he said coyly. "In the choir . . . and at Cliff Bell's, too."

Sparkle could have sworn a little trickle of pee hit her pants. She stopped in her tracks, the fork she was about to place at Mama's place setting rattling in her furiously shaking hand. Just then, Emma entered the room, and her eagle eye zoned right in on Sparkle's trembling hand. "What are you doing, having a seizure over there?" she demanded as she set down the collards on the table. "Set the table. Reverend Bryce has to get back to the church," she added, heading back into the kitchen without giving Sparkle a chance to respond.

Reverend Bryce checked to make sure Emma was out of earshot. "I won't tell your mama if you can get me a table for my birthday," he whispered.

Dolores set a dish on the table, unfazed by Reverend Bryce's demands. "You'll have a nice table for four at the front," she said confidently.

"More like the middle," Reverend Bryce said quickly. "So I blend in."

He smiled triumphantly as Emma reentered the room with Miss Waters and the roast. "Dinner's ready," she said, taking her seat at the table. "Reverend, will you please bless the food?"

Sparkle slid into her seat and put her napkin on her lap. "Sister's not here yet," she said, looking at her watch. "She said she was coming."

"Those who do, do," Emma snapped.

Frankly, Emma was disgusted with Sister, who'd started making a habit of spending the night out of the house with God knows who. She'd even skipped church over the last few Sundays—didn't even show up to the church anniversary, where she was supposed to sing a solo to celebrate its fifteenth year in the building on Clairmount Street. Indeed, in the past week, Emma had seen Sister only twice, and even that was when she was walking out the door. She'd already gone through Sister's suitcases, searching for clues to where she was going and, despite no evidence, quickly came to the conclusion that she was either on drugs, drinking or laying up under some no-account man who'd gotten a hold on her soul. That's all men were good for anyway— at least the ones who were no good. Emma couldn't imagine that Sister could find anything other than a no-good man—not at her age. Not with her reputation. Not with the rumors of what she did while she was in New York.

And now here she was, showing up late to Sunday dinner with the pastor after having skipped church? Emma thought it the height of disrespect, and she wasn't going to waste another second waiting for Sister. "Reverend? Go on ahead and bless the table," she said, curtly.

"Bow your heads," Reverend Bryce said, oblivious to Emma's displeasure.

Everyone around the table—Emma, Sparkle, Dolores, Miss Waters and Tune Ann—settled into their seats and held hands to pray.

"Our Father in Heaven, for this meal you have given, we want to say thank you. Bless the ones who prepared it. And Lord, as we share it, will you stay with us and be our guest of honor. Not just at this meal, but God in our waking, God in our speaking, God in our playing, God in our digesting, God in our working, God in our resting. In a world where so many are hungry, may we eat this food with humble hearts. In a world where so many are lonely, may we share this friendship with joyful hearts."

Revered Bryce took a short pause—a pause long enough for Tune Ann to think the prayer was over. She broke the chain of hands, said a soft "Amen" and reached for the biscuits, until she realized that Reverend Bryce wasn't done. Then she rolled her eyes and rejoined the prayer, drawing a small giggle out of Sparkle.

Reverend Bryce continued with his marathon grace session: "May this food, so fresh and fragrant, call forth reverence for you in our souls. As you give this strength to our perishable limbs, so give us grace for our immortal lives. And let's not forget the blessings on this family. For all the days they've had together and all the days to come. For the joys and sorrows that bind us all ever closer. Lord, we thank you. Amen."

The room broke out into a chorus of "Amens" and lots of serving spoons clinking against dishes, only to be brought to a quick quiet by the sound of a man's voice—crackling loud.

"No wonder black folks can't get ahead," said Satin, who, along with Sister, had quietly and unexpectedly walked into the dining room while everyone's eyes were closed in prayer. Sister was holding his hand; she looked absolutely gorgeous—had in her hair a huge red flower the same shade as her lipstick and a tight red dress that showed off her curvy figure and teeny waist. Every mouth in the room dropped. "It's not because we're lazy. It's because we're so busy praying for our forty acres and a mule, by the time black folks get to 'amen,' the mule is dog food and the forty acres was sold from underneath us because we were too busy praying."

Clearly, Satin meant his comments as a joke, but as usual, no one was laughing. Sister surveyed the room and shifted uncomfortably from one kitten-heeled shoe to the other. Finally, she cleared her throat and broke the ice. "Mom, this is Satin," she said, forcing a smile.

"Pleasure," Emma said. But by the looks of her scowl, clearly, she was far from pleased.

Satin, oblivious to the heat in the room, smiled. "All mine, Ms. Anderson. All mine."

Dolores tossed a look at Sparkle and leaned in. "Two dollars says he doesn't make it to dessert," she whispered.

"Five says he doesn't even get food on his plate," Sparkle whispered back. "Look at Mama's face."

They both looked at their mother; if daggers could shoot from a human's eyes, everyone in the room would have taken cover by now.

Emma folded her hands on her lap and, after a moment more of an icy glare, spoke. "Sister, you and Mr. Struthers have a seat. You're late."

Sister grimaced but didn't answer her mother back—just took Satin by his hand and led him to the two empty seats at the dining room table, introducing him one-by-one to everyone there, even Sparkle and Dee, who, to save their behinds, pretended that they'd never met the man before.

"And this is Reverend Bryce," Sister told Satin as she took a seat next to him.

"Nice to meet you, Reverend," Satin greeted.

Reverend clearly was unimpressed. He, like many in his congregation and throughout Detroit, had a problem with the comedian, whose latest stand-up routine took aim at Negroes for the riots that had swept the city not even a year earlier—a mass civil disturbance that left forty-three people dead, almost 500 people injured, more than 2,000 buildings destroyed and more than 7,000 people arrested for their part in looting and burning down Detroit. Everyone blamed the police for the massive insurrection; after years of suffering at the hands of the brutal, abusive police force, black folk had finally had enough one night when Detroit police offers raided the Blind Pig, a popular but unlicensed nightspot where more than eighty people were celebrating the return of two Negroes from Vietnam. Rather than simply telling everyone to go home, the police proceeded to arrest everyone in the club—everyone!—and they did it with the typical bravado, brashness and nastiness white police officers specialized in extending to black citizens. No one was certain whether Negroes were just fed up or if they were making a political statement to mesh with the power and demands of the Civil Rights Movement, but one thing was for certain: black folks were fed up, and they'd rather tear the whole city down than take one more night of mistreatment from both the crooked racist cops who brutalized their children in their streets and the system that stacked the deck against blacks so that they were stuck with substandard housing, education and medical services, lesser pay and just plain mistreatment by their fellow white Detroiters. And so they looted. And they sent sniper fire out into the streets. And they tried to burn the city down to the ground until the feds sent in the National Guard, armed with tanks and machine guns, treating the streets of Detroit and black Detroiters like they were enemy combatants in their own homeland.

It had been almost a year, but black folk in Detroit were still raw. And they definitely didn't appreciate any black man who made light of the situation by pointing the finger at the reaction of the oppressed instead of the actions of the oppressors.

"Saw you on the TV," he said icily. "You were pretty hard on the folk here in Detroit after the riots."

"I was just telling the truth," Satin said simply. "Shows a lack of intelligence to burn down and loot your own neighborhood. That just makes no sense."

"People were angry," Reverend Bryce countered.

"At white people. So go tear up *their* shit," Satin seethed. "Sorry, excuse me. Hail Mary."

"That's Catholic," Dolores interrupted.

"It's still Christian, right?" Satin snapped. "Look, I understand, but I'm just trying to get black folk to look at it from a different perspective, that's all."

"Burning and looting your own neighborhood may be misguided, but at least those people out there are trying to fight to change the system," Reverend Bryce reasoned. "With all due respect, you're just trying to make a dollar off their pain, brother."

Satin was getting hotter, but he let his reaction simmer

rather than boil. He was, after all, at his girlfriend's mama's dinner table. But he was going to have his say. "Well, you would know better than I about making money off of people's pain," he said, locking eyes with the pastor. "You pack them in every Sunday and give them a show. The difference between me and you is that you collect your fee in the pews and I make sure I get mine at the door."

The entire room feel silent; everyone was uncomfortable, save for Tune Ann, who was too busy eating and slurping to let the argument interrupt her. Miss Waters shot her a look that said *put it down,* but Tune Ann simply took another bite of chicken and chewed more quietly. Emma missed all of that, though; she was too busy glaring at Sister.

"Definitely not making it to dessert," Sparkle whispered, leaning into Dolores.

Satin turned his attention from Reverend Bryce and toward Emma. "Food looks delicious, Ms. Anderson," he said.

Emma didn't bother looking at him. She was too busy sending the death glare in Sister's direction.

Satin ignored the heat coming from the other side of the table. "Well, I guess now is as good a time as any to ask for your daughter's hand in marriage," he rushed.

Emma's icy glare turned into pure anger.

"Surprise," Sister said sweetly, trying to ease the tension in the room. "He asked me last night. Got on one knee, said he couldn't live without me." She wiggled her ring finger around the table so that they could all eyeball the rock Satin had given her after a romantic dinner cooked and served by a chef at his extravagant home. Sister had been taken totally by surprise; she liked the man, sure, and they had their fair share of good times while he showed her the posh life, but when it came to the ladies, Satin was no angel. Of this, Sister was clear. Still, she was more than happy to be his wife—to take his ring as a symbol that this star, who could and did have his way with the most beautiful women in Detroit, put her first. She was good with that.

Emma glowered at Sister. "You want to get married to this man? The way he's disrespecting our house? The Reverend?"

"He's a comedian," Sister giggled, dismissing her mother's anger. "He was trying to make us laugh. Mama, he's a good guy. He even goes to church. Sometimes."

"Granted, it's to get material, but I'm there," Satin said, digging his fork into a piece of chicken in the basket full of the fried meat.

"Stop!" Sister laughed. She turned to her mother. "He tithes."

Emma saw no humor in the moment. At. All.

"I think enough of you to introduce you to doctors and dentists and accountants, but no, you want to ho yourself out to a coon," she seethed.

"Mama!" Sparkle yelled.

Satin cut Emma a look—a look that made clear that if she weren't a woman, it wasn't a Sunday and he wasn't sitting at her dinner table, he would have slapped the mess out of her. And then, the look morphed into a smile. "I'm probably more of a Sambo," he offered. "I do coon it from time to time. But Sambo is my go-to."

Emma ignored Satin; he wasn't worth her breath. "Think better of yourself," she told Sister. "I know you're getting older and worried about who's going to marry you. But honey, get older, don't get desperate."

"Desperate?" Sister said, reeling back. "I'm doing a whole lot better than you ever did. Oh, wait—just keeping a man would be a whole lot better than you did."

Uncomfortable, Reverend Bryce tried to defuse the situation. "Okay, ladies, that's enough," he said, adjusting his seat and patting the table with his fat fingers.

"No," Emma said. "Let her have her attention. She doesn't have much else."

Dolores took a stab at getting the women to stop arguing. "Maybe this is a conversation . . ." she started.

But Sister cut her off. "No, Dee. Me getting a good husband is not about me, it's about her. It's not my fault she got knocked up at sixteen and still wants folks to think that she's the perfect mother—raised some good girls," she said in a raised voice. Then she turned her attention to her mother. "Sparkle's gonna follow up behind you and be a little church mouse and make dresses, and if she's lucky, be a preacher's wife. And you, Dolores, you're going to be a doctor. And I'm just supposed to marry one.

"Funny thing is, maybe I could've snagged one had she sent me to school like you two, but I was raising her kids and picking her up out of her own vomit," Sister continued, seething.

"If you're going to tell my tragic story, do me the honor and get the facts right!" Emma yelled. "I may have passed out, sure. But never did I lay in my own vomit."

Not that Emma would have remembered. She was too drunk, too high, too sad, too oblivious, too far gone to remember much about even that year, let alone that fateful night when she stumbled back into their small apartment in Harlem in the middle of the night, her eye blackened, her lip bleeding, alternately mumbling and yelling curses and swinging at the air. Dolores and Sparkle were too little to remember—just ages six and nine at the time—and they'd long been cuddled up, sleeping on a small mattress in the back room, when Emma finally made her way through the door. Sister was used to their mother staying out at all hours of the night—used to her mother cupping her face in her hands and running down a list of chores Emma wanted her to have finished by the time she pushed her key back in the front door. "Make sure you roll their hair," she'd say. "Feed 'em—there should be something in that refrigerator y'all can eat," she'd snap. "Wash them up and have them in the bed by the time I get back here, or there's going to be trouble," she'd warn. "And you better not open this door for nobody. You hear me? Or they'll come get you—take you away from here."

Sister didn't know who "they" were, but the possibility of someone coming to get her and her sisters sent tremors down her spine. How could she fight "them" and protect her sisters, too? She was, after all, only fourteen—a child. Big for her age, but still, no match for "them." But her mother's addiction—to drugs, to liquor, to men—made Sister grow up. Fast. Scared her, more than anything, into quickly learning how to stretch. How to protect. How to survive. There were plenty of nights that she'd sit her sisters down to bowls of nothing more than grits with a little Karo syrup mixed in for flavor, plenty of nights when she had to sit and make up stories so that her voice could drown out all the scary noises out on the street below their window—the sirens and the fighting and the men calling out to the women and laughing their sinister laughs. And when Dolores and Sparkle slept, Sister would sit, eyes wide-open, too scared to close them until she heard her mother's keys rattling in the door. More often than not, she'd be inebriated. But she'd be home. And Sister could close her eyes until the morning came.

But there would be no sleeping that night. Only Sister's stilted cries, begging her mother to wake up. Begging her to tell her what happened—who beat her and made her bleed and weep uncontrollably. Who muddied and bloodied her beautiful dress, the white one with the rhinestones that she wore when she sang backup for Dolores's daddy.

Her mother was incapable of answering her daughter's questions. Incapable, even, of keeping her eyes open. All Emma could do was stumble and cry out the curses and stumble some more, until, finally, her words were overcome with chunks of throw-up and orange liquid and lots of hurling. And when the contents of her stomach were empty—when there was nothing left but the dry heaving of her stomach—Emma stumbled and fell onto the floor in her own mess, wallowing in it like a pig in slop.

Sister stood there over her mother—her fear replaced by disgust. In the moments that she'd watched her mother there, crawling in her vomit, Tammy Anderson aged into a grown woman—a grown woman with a mission. To get as far away from her mother as she could, as quickly as possible. No good could come from staying there. She had to be . . . free.

"Since the facts are what's so important to you, here are mine," Sister said, staring her mother down. "I was desperate years ago. Right now, I'm just trying to get the hell up out of here and get something besides a color TV and half a room."

No one in the room made a peep. Emma watched as tears welled in her daughter's eyes, but still she sat, stone-faced. It was Tune Ann who broke the silence. "Food's getting cold."

Sister wiped away a tear that escaped from her water-filled eyes. But she kept staring at Emma, too, determined.

"We should probably go," Satin finally said, pushing back from the dining room table. "Thank you, Ms. Anderson, for what looks like would have been a really good dinner."

Emma shot an evil glare at Satin, then turned her attention back to Sister. "You leave my house again, there's no coming back."

And at the sound of those words, Sister got up and walked straight to Sparkle's room without so much as another sound, Sparkle close on her heels.

Satin adjusted his suit jacket and fluffed his pocket square; he didn't bother looking after Sister. "For those who care to come, we're having a June wedding," he said as the rest of the room looked down the hallway, where Sister was loudly tossing all of her things into her suitcases.

Sister had everything packed in minutes; Sparkle

watched her, uncomfortable, struggling to get the words out of her throat and into the air. Finally, she blurted it out: "Are you still going to be a part of the group?"

Sister looked at her little sister, incredulous. "Not what was on my mind, Spark, but yeah. Yeah, sure," she said as she marched out of the room with her bags. She almost ran into Dolores, who was standing in the hallway to meet her sisters.

"Dee? Don't just stand there," Sparkle begged. "Say something."

Dee simply reached out and hugged her sister. Oddly, she was proud of Sister—knew that her sister couldn't stay caged in their mother's house without losing her soul. "Congratulations," she said.

Dolores and Sister hugged one another harder and cried a little in each other's arms. And then, almost as quickly as the hug began, it ended, with Sister pulling away, regaining her composure, kissing Dee's forehead and then Sparkle's, and marching past the dining room and out the front door. Satin tipped his hat and followed her out.

Sparkle, unable to hold back her tears, ran back into her room and tossed herself on her bed. Her sister was gone. Again.

Later, after their company had left and Mama and Dolores cleaned up their place, Sparkle snuck into her mother's room and called Levi's place, looking for Stix. She crossed her fingers as the phone rang, praying that he was there to answer. There to save her. When she heard his voice on the other end of the line, she let out an audible exhale. "Can you meet me at our spot at ten o'clock?" she rushed.

"Wait, what? Sparkle?"

"Can you meet me at ten o'clock?" she demanded.

"Sparkle, what's wrong? Tell me what's going on," Stix said.

"Sister is gone. With Satin," Sparkle said, and then, more loudly: "She's gone."

Stix was quiet.

"Look, I have to go. Just meet me at ten o'clock. Our spot."

"Okay," he said. "See you there."

And when Sparkle had snuck out the side door of her house, made her way down the street and saw Stix waiting on his motorcycle, she finally felt like she could breathe again.

"Where you want to go?" Stix asked as he watched Sparkle slip on her shoes.

"Anywhere," she said as she climbed onto the back of the motorcycle.

She said not another word for the rest of the night; she just held Stix tightly as he maneuvered through the city, the lights passing them by. And as she laid her head against his back, she knew for sure, as did he, that there was nowhere else either of them wanted to be.

# CHAPTER 8

Sister was supposed to be in the shoe department at Hudson's—greeting the customers, helping them sort through the latest styles of sandals and kitten heels, and escorting them to the register so that they could pay for their purchases. But she hated her job—the way the white women flaunted their excess as they ordered her around and deliberately mistreated the black girls who worked at the department store. Sister bristled every time one of them snapped at her; rarely, if ever, did they ask for help nicely. It was always, "Come here, gal, and get this one in a size eight," and "Come here, gal—make yourself useful and help me get these shoes onto my feet." On more than a few occasions, they just outright called her "nigger"—a couple of times because she couldn't find the shoes they liked in the right size, a few more times just because that's what their mama, and their mama's mama, called Negroes and that was what they were going to call Negroes, too. A few of the other black women in the department store just shrugged it off—pretended as if they didn't hear it or held their tongue by silently reminding themselves that if it were not for that paycheck from Hudson's, they'd be off somewhere scrubbing somebody's toilet or mopping people's floors or washing their dirty drawers and working from sunup to can't-see for even less pay than they were getting at the store. But Sister? Her strength was fast fading. She simply couldn't reconcile being hired because she was a light-skinned, pretty woman—the only kind of Negroes that ever got hired for positions out in the front of the store working with customers—with being treated as if she were nothing more than some animal.

And her man felt the same way. So he made her skip work—pulled her back down into the bed and showered her with a thousand kisses when she tried to get up and get ready for her shift. "My woman doesn't need to work," he said as he ran his hands down the length of her body and then covered her frame with his own. "Papa's going to take care of you. Papa's going to take real good care of you."

And Sister let him. Happily. It was, after all, what she wanted: to be with a man who could take her places, show her things—make life easier. Satin didn't care about her past—didn't care about her evil mama or the mess she'd made in New York. He didn't even care that she wanted to be with him because of his fame and money. He was used to these things—expected it, even. What woman didn't want to follow the money? The clothes? The celebrity? The lifestyle? Sister was perfect for him—had a little grime on her and a little bit of fame, too. Plus, she was fine as hell.

And sexy. For Satin, there was no downside. He just had to work with her a little bit.

"Come here, baby," Sister said to Satin as she pulled his arm. He could have slept another couple of hours—it had been a long night thanks to his new fiancée—but he had a hunger. It was calling him. So Satin took her hand and let Sister lead him into the dining room. "I got a surprise for you," she said. "Sit down and close your eyes."

Satin tied his robe, sat back in the chair at the mahogany dining table and did as he was told. He could hear Sister toiling away with something in the kitchen and then making her way back over to him and setting something on the table. "Okay, open them," she ordered.

Satin opened his eyes to a simple cup of coffee—black and sweet, the way he liked it. Sister beamed, proud of herself for learning how to work the fancy coffee machine Satin had in his huge kitchen, the likes of which Sister had never seen. She'd, of course, been with her fair share of men with means. But waking up and having full access to the kitchen—and making breakfast for them—was never on the agenda. Usually, they got what they wanted and then showed her to the door, well before the sun rose. Satin was different, though; he paid attention to her, lavished her with fine things, made her the center of attention around all of his friends and hangers-on. In the few weeks that they'd been together, Satin had made Sister the very center of his world—always introduced her as his "lady," and pulled out chairs for her and held her hand as his boys shuffled off to swing the car around. He even mushed a girl in her head for making a scene at Cliff Bell's when he told her to get up from his table so that Sister could sit. Sister could have done without him calling the girl a bitch, and she definitely thought that putting his hands on her was overkill, but she had to admit: she felt safe and protected and loved when Satin made clear to anyone within the sound of his voice that he belonged to Tammy Anderson and Tammy Anderson belonged to him.

"Your cup of coffee, sir," she said. The two of them laughed as she straddled him in the chair. "I take care of my man."

Satin reached up and kissed Sister. Deeply. Passionately.

"I appreciate it, baby," he said, smiling. "But Papa needs to wake up a little faster and a little stronger."

Satin, his eyes locked with Sisters's, reached into his robe pocket and pulled out a waxed paper packet full of white powder. He reached for her right hand, slowly opened it, kissed her palm, and then laid a line of cocaine in it. With one long snort, he made the line disappear.

"Stick out your tongue," he said to Sister.

She did as she was told; he took her hand with the residue on it and slowly dragged it across her tongue. "Wait till you see what it does when we make love," he said, gently laying her across the table.

Sister was quite familiar with the drug—she'd witnessed its power firsthand during her time in New York. She'd seen what it did to her roommate when her boyfriend pumped it into her. It got a hold of her something terrible, but in Sister's mind, it was only because the drug was forced on her. Sister's boyfriend didn't fly. He kept control over his girlfriends with his voice. With his fists. He only had to hit Sister but one time for her to do as she was told, but the moment she was able to plot and make her escape, she was out of there. Her wings were too big to be clipped by a man who was only using her. Who didn't love her.

Satin was different. He did love her—was crazy about his Sister. And a line or two wasn't going to change that. It wasn't going to change him. Of this, Sister was certain.

Sparkle wasn't sure about anything. Stix was almost impossible to read; she couldn't tell if he liked her or if he just liked being in business with her. Those were two separate and distinct things, for sure, but Stix expertly mixed the two like a church lady does a southern lemon pound cake for after Sunday service. It was much too easy for him to run hot and then cold, to be loving and then demanding, to act like Sparkle was his girl and then act like she was nothing more than his client. Sparkle hadn't seen any evidence of him dating anyone else—no women ever showed up to the club looking to sit at his table, and though she'd seen plenty of them vie for his attention, he never paid them much mind or gave them a reason to think they had a shot with him.

But when they were alone—just Stix and Sparkle—she didn't know what to do to show him that she wanted more. She'd never had a boyfriend—had never been kissed until Stix came along and laid it on her. She was shy. Pretty but plain. And it didn't help at all that she was the little sister of Sister, one of the prettiest girls in town, and the daughter of Emma, one of the meanest women in the Midwest. Guys just knew better than to try. Even the ones that Sparkle thought she might want to give a shot.

But these days, she only had eyes for Stix.

Sparkle peeked at him from behind the dressing-room curtain at her mother's dress shop, trying her best not to let him see her checking him out. It was the third time that week that she'd convinced Stix to slip away with her into the night so that she could get some air—get away from Mama's anger over Sister, get away from Dolores, who kept trying to rationalize Sister leaving, get her mind off Sister not being there with her anymore. Stix happily obliged Sparkle's requests. On this particular night, Sparkle had directed him to her mother's dress shop. She'd been watching her mother whip up dresses for a few new clients—beautiful gowns they'd planned to wear to a popular pageant and cotillion coming up in a few weeks—and she was dying to play dress-up in the frocks. Mama would kill her with her bare hands if she knew she was in the shop with a boy, messing with her clients' clothes, but that didn't stop her from getting a little daring that night.

Stix was lying on the floor, using a bolt of fabric for a pillow, when he called out to Sparkle: "What are you doing in there? Hurry up!"

"Stop rushing me, please," Sparkle insisted.

"You're the one sneaking into your mama's store," Stix said, adjusting the fabric to get more comfortable as he peered around the dimly lit store. "Ooh, you're a bad girl, Sparkle Anderson," he teased.

"Shut up," Sparkle laughed as she opened the curtain and stepped out of the dressing room. She smoothed down the sequined red gown and adjusted the straps on her shoulders before she looked up at Stix, beaming. This dress, she knew, was even more fabulous than the three others she'd tried on. She could tell by the sly smile Stix was giving her.

"Beautiful," he said.

"Not too sexy?" she asked, looking down at her body, alternately admiring and being embarrassed by how the dress showed off her curves.

"Well, let me see. Model it for me."

Sparkle hesitated, and, instinctively, looked out over the front of the store nervously.

"Don't act like you're new to sneaking around," Stix laughed. "Come on, we're here now. If we get busted, at least let's say we had some fun."

Sparkle let out the breath she'd been holding and smiled. He was right. So she hopped up on her toes and worked the room like a model, swishing back and forth in front of Stix like she owned the floor. Within a few steps, though, she got shy and started doing the Funky Chicken to draw attention away from her sexiness. Both of them laughed at her silliness.

"Now take it off," Stix said suggestively.

Sparkle's heart leaped. She was cool with the kissing, but was Stix really trying to get her to make love? Sparkle wanted his full attention, but she certainly wasn't ready for that. She needed to know he was worthy of something so special. So sacred. She wasted no time letting him know it.

"Someone once told me that they love you more when you make them pay," she said, folding her arms across her chest to hide her breasts, which, at that precise moment, in that dress, felt absolutely naked. "As my mother would say, 'Your currency is time and I need more of it.'"

Stix smirked. "Look at you, putting me in my place," he said. "But I still need you to take the dress off."

"Stix, for real," she said angrily. "Don't pressure me."

Stix fell out in laughter. "Girl, you got mad quick. I need you to take it off so you can keep it nice," he said. "I thought you could wear it when you and your sisters . . ." he started, holding Sparkle in suspense.

"What, Stix?" she asked, getting a little excited.

"When you and your sisters open up for Aretha Franklin at the Fillmore!" he exclaimed.

Sparkle shook her head as if rattling her brain would make her hear more correctly. Because clearly, she thought, she must have mistaken what Stix had just told her. "What?" she asked.

"Baby, you're opening up for Aretha!" he said, hopping up and rushing over to hug Sparkle.

"Don't lie to me, Stix!" Sparkle said, grabbling his hands and jumping around in circles.

"I ain't lying!"

Sparkle let out a scream and the two jumped up and down in celebration, as if they were the only two people in the world who mattered. Sister and Her Sisters had come quite far from their days of making up songs and dances in their mother's piano room, but this, Sparkle didn't see coming. Opening up for the Queen of Soul herself. It was almost too much for Sparkle to handle.

In fact, Stix had a hard time wrapping his mind around it, too. He knew getting the girls to open for a major headliner at the Fillmore would be no easy feat, particularly considering that getting the manager, Fred Davies, to see new acts was akin to getting Jesus Christ himself to come have a drink at the local bar. Davies had an ear for talent, but staked the concert hall's claim on booking only the best for his stage—entertainers who could pack in a crowd in the two-story venue and leave the audience so mesmerized, so tired from dancing and sore from shouting, that they'd talk about the show for months later and clamor to get a ticket when they came back to town. Simply put: Davies didn't do locals who anyone with a couple of bucks and a little time on their hands could see on any given night in a hole-in-the-wall club in Detroit.

But Davies had heard about this group—had seen the excitement they inspired in the workers who came to the Fillmore talking about the three sisters who were tearing up the stage over at Cliff Bell's. And when Stix swung by his offices to invite—well, beg—Davies to come check out Sister and Her Sisters, Davies just so happened to be thinking about doing just that.

Stix didn't tell Sparkle, Sister and Dolores about his attempts at getting them on the Fillmore stage because he was fully aware of what a long shot it would be and he didn't want to get them all amped, only to be shut down. He didn't even mention that Davies had agreed to stop by and catch one of their sets, out of fear that he wouldn't show up or that the girls would get nervous knowing he was in the audience checking them out.

But Stix knew that if, by some miracle, Davies showed up to Cliff Bell's to see Sister do her thing up on that stage, he'd be hooked. One look at Sister doing her thing—batting those eyelashes, using that come-hither finger and those sexy shimmies to suck the crowd in—and Davies would think about whether he should have Aretha open up for Sister.

And when Davies showed up at the last Cliff Bell's show, hiding by the bar behind a crowd of big girls, sipping on a spritzer with a twist of lime, Stix knew he had him. Just knew it by the way Davies stared at that stage and the crowd's reaction to what was going on up there like he was watching piles of cash float through the air. Davies could smell the money. Taste it. And Stix knew it.

He didn't rush Davies at the club to get a commitment. Indeed, Stix didn't even go by the Fillmore to ask him what his decision was. Instead, he waited by the phone for two days for Davies to give him a ring, barely leaving for food or bathroom breaks out of fear that he'd miss the call. He collapsed in a heap, too, when Davies finally did dial his number to extend the good news: Sister and Her Sisters would open for Aretha Franklin's one-night-only performance.

Sparkle was the first one he told; he wanted to share the good news with her because, well, he adored her. Adored what they had together. Doing right by her, her music and her group was the only way he knew how to show it.

"You are really going to have to dig deep and pull out the best song you've ever written," he said as Sparkle collapsed into his arms, giddy.

"I have it already," she said. "I wrote it the night you first kissed me."

"I can't wait to hear it," he smiled.

"You will, the night I open up for Aretha Franklin!" she said, stomping her feet excitedly.

And when she looked into Stix's eyes, she knew what they had was real—even if he never said it. She pushed her man back down to the floor, sat on his lap and boldly gave Stix a deep, passionate kiss. Something he could feel.

# CHAPTER 9

SPARKLE, SISTER AND Dolores had only a few weeks to get ready for their show at the Fillmore, and Sparkle and Dolores had to squeeze in practices while holding down jobs and hiding their dresses, new music, practice sessions and neighborhood excitement over their big break from their mother. A couple of times, they almost got busted when, right in front of Mama, some of the younger choir and Bible study members asked them whether they could score free tickets to the concert. "I mean, since we've been close and all, singing in this choir together for how many years?" Laurene asked, all loud, at the last Bible study. "That's got to be worth a ticket to see you guys up on the stage with Aretha. I'll even take seats way up in the back and at the top," she begged. Dolores shot her a death glare that sent shivers down Laurene's spine, with just enough time to spare as Mama made her way back into the living room with her Bible study guide, ready to start the lessons. Sparkle, never one to be all that good at breaking the rules and being sneaky, almost fainted of fear thinking her mother overheard Laurene's plea and spent the rest of the hour trembling, despite Dolores's silent pleas for her to pull herself together.

But Sparkle was in full control when she was playing her music and practicing with her sisters, especially when she had no fear of Mama walking in on them. That was why she loved practicing at Sister's place. Satin's house was humongous—certainly befitting a man who made such a fine living as an entertainer. There was so much space in the middle of their living room that the girls barely had to move any of the furniture around to practice their dance moves, and Satin had a fine piano that, despite its tuning issues, Sparkle enjoyed playing while they rehearsed the songs and their harmonies. Every chance they got, the girls piled into that living room and ran their numbers as if they were about to perform for their lives.

"Come on, Sparkle," Dolores giggled as her sister bumped into her—again—while they ran through new-and-improved steps for their song "Hooked on Your Love." "I swear, your two left feet are going to have us falling over the stage of the Fillmore."

The sisters laughed; it was the running joke that Sparkle, the one with enough musical talent to rival all of Berry Gordy's songwriting teams put together, couldn't dance a lick, and every time they had the chance to, which was often, they made fun of Sparkle's two left feet. Sister laughed the hardest, then sniffled as if she was on the verge of getting sick.

"You catching a cold?" Dolores asked, concerned.

Sister hesitated, trying to figure out a lie about her runny nose. Truly, her sniffles had nothing to do with the stash of hot air that had swept over Detroit. But there was no way she was going to explain to her sisters the effects her cocaine use was taking on her nose, which seemed to always be running, bleeding or plain not working right. Satin saved her from having to fib to her sisters when he poked his head out of their bedroom door.

"Y'all ain't got to go home, but you know the rest," he snapped, looking a mess. His conk was greasy and hanging off his head at an impossibly odd angle, surpassed in weirdness only by his wrinkled, stained T-shirt, which looked like it hadn't been changed in a few days. Dolores, who had a nose like a wolf, could smell him all the way in the living room.

The lighthearted mood the sisters shared changed instantly as Satin crossed to the bar to pour himself a scotch. Dolores and Sparkle exchanged "oops" faces as Sister shifted from one foot to the other, wiping her nose and looking nervous.

"They were just leaving," Sister said nervously, more to her sisters than to her man. Sparkle and Dee didn't need any more cues; they immediately gathered their purses and sheet music and got ready to head on out the door. "Baby," Sister said, turning to Satin, "can you give them some cab fare?"

Satin drained the scotch out of his glass and started pouring himself another. "You the one with all the money," he snapped, as the brown liquid splashed against the crystal. "About to open up for Aretha Franklin. If I had any sense, I'd be living off of *you*."

Sparkle didn't find what Satin was saying funny by any stretch, but she laughed out loud, hoping that a little light-hearted giggle would ease the tension.

"You think I'm funny?" Satin smiled.

"Yeah," Sparkle said, smiling back.

"So you're laughing along with those white folks I 'coon' for?" he asked, this time, his words more sinister.

"No," Sparkle answered nervously.

"Satin," Sister interjected. She could see where this was going, and she was desperate to shut it down before Satin got out of hand.

Satin was unmoved. "Well, you *should* be laughing," he seethed. "That's how I pay for all this heat you're suck-ing up around here."

"Satin, I'm . . ." Sparkle stammered.

"Just go," Sister insisted, gently taking Sparkle by the shoulder and motioning to Dolores to head toward the door.

Satin gave the girls one final glare, took a sip of his scotch, and slinked back into the bedroom, with Sister eyeing him until he slammed the door behind him. When she was sure he was in the room for good, she grabbed her purse off the back of the dining room chair and pulled out a crisp ten-dollar bill. "Here," she said to no one in particu-lar as she waved the money in the air and sniffled.

"Everything okay?" Dolores asked, watching Sister closely.

"It's fine. Everything is fine," Sister said, forcing a smile to her face. "Men are just like babies, you know? Cranky when they're hungry and sleepy. Which is exactly what we need. Sleep. We have to open up for Ms. Franklin tomorrow."

Sister smiled a little harder, which made her sisters smile, too. Sparkle and Dolores took turns hugging Sister and saying their goodbyes. "Get home safe, hear?" she called after them as they walked down the front stoop and across the front yard.

Sister's smile faded as she closed the door and locked it.

And then, before she could fully turn around, a blizzard of punches, pushes and slaps rained down on Sister—knuckle collided with eye, head slammed against door, open palm connected with cheek, their quickness and severity so shocking she couldn't catch her breath.

"Told you about bringing those bitches over here to my living room making all that noise," Satin said, his fingers squeezing Sister's neck so hard she couldn't get a word out if she tried. "Hell is wrong with you?" he yelled, giving Sister a final push before releasing his grip. His fingers had been so tight that his fingerprints practically shined on Sister's delicate, peach-colored skin. She coughed and clutched at her neck, trying to breathe between the sobs that overcame her.

Satin wrapped his fingers into Sister's pink cashmere sweater—a gift he'd bought her the day that he accompanied her over to Hudson's to tell her boss she was quitting and that he should kiss her black ass—and pulled Sister, crumpled in a fetal position to guard herself from her fiancé's blows, to her feet. "As much as I got on my mind, trying to find a way to make some money off these crackers, you gonna bring those loud-ass sisters of yours into my house, interrupting my thoughts and my sleep, too?"

"I'm sorry," Sister said, stuttering. "Satin, please—I'm sorry."

"Shut the hell up while I'm talking," he yelled, smacking her in her head with one hand while he pulled her with the other.

Sister knew this was coming—could smell it on Satin's breath, see it in his eyes. She wasn't a doctoral candidate but she was perceptive—had this uncanny ability to feel danger when it was headed her way, particularly at the hands of men. After almost two months of living with him, she definitely understood Satin's triggers. The edge and bite that attracted her to him, that had seeped rather quickly into their young relationship, was the same that had turned him against her. First, Satin got a little gruff with her because she woke up too early for his tastes and made too much noise while she was in the bathroom. She tried to explain to him that she'd gotten her monthly and needed to get up and put on her pad and fix herself a little tea to settle her cramps, but he wasn't trying to hear it. "This ain't your mama's house—we're not doing slave hours, rising before sunrise to pick the cotton," he snapped. "I'm the massah, and massah says stay your ass in the bed until I tell you to get up."

A few days after that, he grabbed her by the back of her neck at Dalvin's for questioning who, exactly, was the woman who'd joined their table at dinner. Sister's question was innocent enough; she thought maybe Ham had finally broken down and got him a woman to look after, seeing as he spent the majority of his waking hours hanging up under Satin. It hadn't occurred to her that the woman was there at the invitation of Satin. "You not paying the bill, you not worrying about who all is sitting at my table," he said, grabbing Sister's neck as they stood outside the restaurant waiting for Ham to pull the car around. The other woman smirked as Sister rubbed her neck where Satin's fingers had squeezed her. Still, Sister found herself more upset that that heifer was climbing in her man's car and laughing at her than she was that Satin had invited her in.

The first slap? That came when she wouldn't hurry off the phone, talking to Sparkle about the gig with Aretha. He'd waited until she hung up, so Sparkle didn't hear, but Sister did have to sneak and call her sister back with an excuse for why she couldn't get together later that night to rehearse. His handprint was still visible, and Sister couldn't bear to explain it to Sparkle and Dolores. Hell, she could barely reconcile it for herself.

The first big-ass whooping—that one came when she was out lounging by the pool, singing Sparkle's new song and dipping her feet in the water, trying to give Satin his privacy as he finished talking to his manager. Sister couldn't be sure—she didn't want Satin to know she was eavesdropping on his phone conversation—but it sounded like plans for his big tour to a bunch of major white establishments out on the East Coast in New York, Boston and Delaware had been cancelled, with no explanation for why they no longer wanted their Golden Negro on their stages. "That's all my money, man!" Satin yelled into the phone. "You need to fix this. I can't make no money slumming it in these little nigga-ass clubs. Do your job!" he said, slamming the phone into the receiver.

Sister, anxious to defuse the situation and calm Satin down, knew she couldn't sit there at the pool humming and twinkling her toes in the water. She needed to do something—something to make him feel good. And quickly. So she dried off her feet, wrapped the towel around herself and, when he walked into the bathroom, made her way to the bedroom. She was pouring a line on his special mirror when Satin walked into the room and accused her of stealing his cocaine.

"What the hell are you doing?" he demanded, his shadow filling the doorway.

"I . . . I was fixing you up a little something, baby," she said, trying to sound more sweet than scared.

"'I . . . I . . .' Why the hell you stuttering?" he asked, moving closer to her, snarling. "The only time people stutter is when they're preparing a lie. Now I'm going to ask you again, why you in my stash?"

"I heard you talking and I wanted to do something to make you feel better," she said, trying her best to make her words clear and concise.

"So you were eavesdropping on my conversation and in here in my stash? What, you trying to get yours before this money dries up?" he said, moving closer.

Sister was so focused on making sure she didn't stutter that she hadn't noticed Satin loosening his belt buckle. With one swift move, he whipped the leather strap from his pants and snapped it across Sister's lower back. Thankfully, the thick terry-cloth towel blocked the sting, but that was just the first blow. The second and the third and the fourth hit her on her upper thigh and calves, and as she tried to escape those, she dropped the towel and ran, leaving her back exposed to the leather's lick.

"Please, Satin, stop!" she pleaded. "Baby, I'm sorry!"

She'd been apologizing a lot lately, for even the most minor of indiscretions. But her words, stilted, hollow, just seemed to escalate Satin's abuse. And so mostly, she'd learned to cater to his every whim—to anticipate his needs before he even realized he was in need—to keep him happy. The three things in the world that made Satin happy? Cocaine, attention and sex. Sister made a point of keeping the three plentiful when Satin was involved.

But now, even that wouldn't save her ass.

"Baby, wait," she said sweetly through her grimacing as Satin pulled her through the house. "Let me do something to make you feel good. Let me get you some candy," she said.

"I got some candy all right," he said. "Yeah, Papa got something for that ass."

And with that, Satin shoved Sister onto their bed and closed the bedroom door behind him. No one could hear her screams but God.

# CHAPTER 10

SPARKLE AND DOLORES loved *Julia*. There was just something extraordinary about sitting down in front of a color TV set and seeing a black woman, the beautiful Diahann Carroll, strutting all that chocolate across the screen, representing for colored folk right there in the living rooms of every American household. The show was centered around her character—her life—and Julia wasn't shucking and jiving to make herself seen and heard. She wasn't birthing no babies, either. There weren't any *yes'ms* falling from her lips, she wasn't scrubbing anybody's toilets and her uniform didn't come with an apron. Julia was a nurse. A nurse who made Negroes who understood the significance of showing black folks in a middle-class existence rather than the degradation of the inner city quite proud.

Sparkle would never forget the night the half-hour prime-time show debuted on the NBC network. In Negro communities stretched all across America, that night was an event for black folk, who so rarely saw themselves on TV that whenever there was word that a black person would be on a television program—like Nat King Cole on *The Dinah Shore Show*, or Diana Ross and the Supremes on *American Bandstand*, or Satin on *The Smothers Brothers Comedy Hour*—everybody literally made appointments to watch. The debut of *Julia* actually inspired parties—with people showing up to each other's houses with cakes and chips and soda and party dresses and dates to watch Diahann Carroll make history. And no matter who they were or what they were doing, every black person in the neighborhood with access to a television watched the show faithfully each week, Mama included.

This is what Sister and Dolores were counting on that particular night. They needed Mama to wrap things up at the dress shop, cook the dinner, clean the dishes, order them around a little and then clear her schedule, shut off the phone and get comfortable in front of the color TV to watch *Julia* because it was pretty much the only way that they were going to be able to get Dolores's spiked tea into her so that they could sneak off to the Fillmore for their big concert debut with Aretha Franklin. Sparkle tried to pay attention to the show—that little Corey, Julia's son, was such a cutie—but her peripheral vision was trained on Mama. Or rather, Mama's coffee mug. Within moments of her drinking down the last sips, Mama was toast. The coffee mug fell gently to the carpet as Mama lay back on the sofa. She was knocked all the way out.

"You want some more tea, Mama?" Dolores said, pushing Mama's arm to see if she'd respond. "Mama?" She got nothing. Sparkle, who'd been sitting on the easy chair, got up and tiptoed over to the couch next to Dolores and the two of them leaned in, each searching Mama's bosom for signs that she was still breathing, and waiting to see if their hot breath on her face would make her open her eyes.

She was alive. And she wouldn't be waking up anytime soon. The coast was clear.

Without another word, the sisters tiptoed down the hallway, leaving their mother on the couch with the TV on. Within fifteen minutes, their hair was laid, their makeup was beat and they were poured into the hot red gowns Stix had presented to them for their big performance. Five minutes after that, they were rolling Emma's car down the driveway and taking off down the road, a rush of emotions—giddiness, fear, excitement, confidence—overcoming them as they made their way to the theater. Stix was in rare form; with all of the talking and bragging and encouraging and demands, you would have thought Muhammad Ali had found his way into Emma's Ford.

"It's on now," he said, slapping his lap as he navigated Emma's car to the back of the building, where the talent was directed to arrive. There, just a few feet away from the door, was a huge bus with *Aretha* written in fancy brown letters on the side—the prettiest thing Sparkle ever did see. And the scariest. Sparkle was pretty amped right up until she saw Aretha's name; no matter how confident she was about her songs and the group's act, there was no denying that opening for the Queen of Soul in their hometown was going to change their lives—or ruin them if they messed up.

"Sister and Her Sisters, about to tear the stage down!"

Stix was yelling, oblivious to Sparkle's fear. "Aretha, Diana—all of them better step aside and take notes."

Sparkle's legs nearly buckled beneath her as she, Dolores, and Stix climbed out of the car and made their way to the back entrance. A big, burly white man in an ill-fitting suit opened the door for them after Stix laid a few quick pounds on the metal; after Stix announced who they were, and the big guy checked his clipboard, the man stepped aside to let them into the back hallway and led them into the dressing room.

"Here we go, ladies—the big time," Stix said, surveying the dressing-room door, which held a plaque that read "Sister and Her Sisters." Inside, there were three dressing tables and humongous mirrors encircled by bright stage lights that were blinding if you looked into them too long. Another table held a bowl of mints, tea, coffee, sandwiches and cookies, all of which would have immediately been gobbled up by Sparkle if she weren't convinced that whatever she swallowed at that very moment would quickly make its way to the floor and onto her pretty new shoes. "Come on, I need you guys to get pumped. Let's go! Put your game faces on!"

"Stix, you're making me nervous," Sparkle said, placing her hands on his shoulders to settle him.

"I'm just trying to get my clients to focus," Stix said, still hopping around the room like he was two beats away from hearing the bell in a heavyweight title bout.

"What you need to be focused on, Mr. Manager, is that one of your clients isn't here," Dolores said coolly.

Stix stopped still and looked around the room as if Sister was going to magically appear in one of its corners or under the table. "Well, where is she?" he said, staring at his watch. "We go on in a half hour. I specifically told her to be here at seven thirty. Did you talk to her?"

"We called before we left the house but there was no answer," Sparkle said. "We figured she and Satin left already."

Worried, Stix started pacing the room, alternately watching the door and looking at his watch, making the girls even more nervous. Sparkle and Dolores tried to ease their minds by powdering their noses and fiddling with the cookies, but they were too nervous to eat. And a little scared of what would happen if Sister didn't show up for the most important date of their musical lives.

Finally, by the time Stix had gnawed off his nails practically to the nub and used the house phone to put in three calls to Satin's house, the girls kicked both of the boys out of the dressing room, and Sparkle and Dolores's stomachs were practically numb with raw nerves, Sister walked into the dressing room with just five minutes to spare before showtime. She didn't say a word—not even "hello." Sparkle and Dolores stood still and just stared at her as she sat at a mirror and slowly, methodically, pulled her makeup out of her bag and placed it on the dressing-room table.

"Uh, hello? Today ain't the day to be fashionably late," Dolores said, breaking the silence.

"You have time," Sparkle added nervously. "Stix says Ms. Franklin's running late. Not even in her dressing room yet."

Sister took off her coat and tossed it over the back of her chair.

"I'm a little worried, though, because that's going to cut it too close getting back home before Mama wakes . . ."

Sparkle's words dissolved into silence when Sister removed her hat and looked into the mirror. There, in the reflection, Sparkle saw a huge welt on her sister's forehead and black-and-blue marks on her jaw. Sparkle's face slowly crinkled into a look of horror. "What happened to your face?" she practically whispered.

"It ain't nothing," Sister said simply as she rubbed a makeup pad into her foundation.

Dolores walked over and grabbed Sister by the chin, turning her face toward hers. "Did he do that to you?" she demanded.

"I had an accident," Sister said, snatching her face out of Dolores's hand and turning back toward the mirror.

"Oh, so, what? You tripped and hit his fist?" Dolores snapped angrily.

"Get out of here!" Sister yelled.

"What?" Dolores said, incredulous.

"You heard me!" Sister said, giving the attitude back to Dolores in spades.

"He's beating you and you're mad at *me*?" Dolores asked, tossing her hands on her hips.

"I said, get out!" Sister said, jumping to her feet and pointing her sister to the door.

Dolores and Sister stood nose-to-nose, seething and huffing like they were going to come to blows. Sparkle's heart was beating so hard she could barely think straight, much less jump between them or say the words that needed to be said to calm the two down. She was too mesmerized by the bruises on Sister's face.

Finally, Dolores backed down and stomped out of the dressing room, disappearing down the hallway. Sister sat down again and reached for her makeup case; out of it, she pulled a dollar bill and carefully unfolded it to reveal a small heap of white powder. Sister used an open matchbook to scoop the white powder out of the dollar bill, brought it to her nose and sniffed hard. She rubbed what was left on her finger and dragged it across her gums.

Sparkle thought she was going to hyperventilate. "What are you doing?" she asked, her chest heaving. "Sister, please tell me that's not . . ."

Sister cut her off, but instead of looking into her eyes, she looked down at her lap. "We got to open up for Aretha Franklin tonight, right?" she asked.

"Right," Sparkle answered softly.

"Yeah, well, Sister can't fly on one wing."

Crushed, Sparkle looked at her sister through the mirror. She had no words. She simply reached down and kissed her big sister on her head and slowly backed out the dressing-room door.

It was the sound of the horns, loud and brash, that woke up Emma from her deep sleep. She slowly opened her eyes and tried to focus, but her vision was blurred and she was a bit disoriented—felt like a grown man had stomped her in her forehead with an old pair of steel-toed brogans. Slowly, she sat up and rubbed her head. "Sparkle?" she called out. "Dolores? Where y'all at? My God, my head," she said, rubbing her temples. After a couple of beats, she looked up, wondering why neither of her daughters had come when she called.

Still dizzy, Emma braced herself as she rose from the couch; each step she took was slow, deliberate. And made her head pound even more. But when she called out her daughters' names again, and there was no answer, Emma knew instinctively that something was going on—something sinister.

She peeked into Dolores's room first. The light was off, but everything was in its place—bed made, bureau clean, carpet vacuumed, schoolwork and books stacked neatly. Emma thought about searching through her drawers and such for clues as to where her daughters might have snuck off to, but she knew Dolores was the sneaky one of the bunch—the one who would be most likely to cover her tracks. But Sparkle? Sloppy. Goody two-shoes. Afraid of her own shadow. Those would be the three characteristics Emma would toss out if someone asked her to describe her youngest daughter. Emma had no doubt that if her girls were up to no good, she could find a clue about what they were doing and where in the sloppy, scared, brown-noser's room.

Emma turned on Sparkle's light and headed for the bureau drawers first, snatching each one open quickly and with great force. Old papers, a few *Jet* magazines, some hair clips—they were all in abundance. But no clues. She snatched open the closet next. Nothing. The purses hanging on the back of her door revealed little—there was gum, a few loose coins, a church program with a number scribbled on it and the word "Stix." She'd heard that name before, but couldn't place where.

A dull thud seized her head as she turned her attention to the bed. She thought twice about getting down on her knees to look under it; her head hurt her so much when she moved it that the mere thought of bending over to take a peek and then getting back up made it hurt that much more. As she tried to decide if it was worth it, Emma noticed something strange about the bed. Sparkle never was good about making it up in the military style her mother had taught her, so it was always a bit more lumpy than Emma cared for it to be. But there was something about the bulge on the right side of the bedspread that caught her eye.

Emma rubbed her neck and squinted a bit, then headed over to the bed to give it a little tossing. With one expert tug, she pulled back the bedspread and sheet; there wasn't anything on the actual mattress, but there was a stray piece of fabric—something that didn't match the sheet or bedspread—hanging from between the mattress and the box spring.

Emma gave the fabric a little tug, but it didn't budge. She pulled out the fitted sheet, but still couldn't make out what it was. Finally, she found the strength to lift the mattress just a little, a move that revealed what looked like the hem of a sleeve. Emma wrinkled her brow and then braced herself against the bed as she flipped the top mattress up and then over the side of the bed.

*Busted.*

"These little heiffas," she muttered under her breath as her eyes swept across four dresses, each one prettier, fancier and sexier than the last—a sunlight-yellow number with sparkles on the neckline and sleeves; an orange swirl-print minidress with a V-neck that would have all of Sparkle's little chest out; a slinky, silver affair with a slit up the side that looked as if she made one wrong move, anyone looking would be able to see what her future-born children would look like, and a peach print dress that looked just like one she'd seen in Miss Peach's Boutique.

Emma snatched all four of the dresses as if they'd done her wrong and headed straight for the living room, her head pounding with every step. Her fingers trembled as she picked up the phone and dialed Sara's number. Sara picked up on the third ring, but didn't have a chance even to say hello before Emma went in on her. "Sara, tell that daughter of yours to stop eating and tell you where my daughters are performing tonight."

Sara looked at the receiver, then turned toward the kitchen table, where, sure enough, Tune Ann was digging into a heaping plate of pinto beans and neck bones with a block of corn bread. She was mid-suck on a neck bone when her mother sighed and blurted out in Tune Ann's direction, "Where are the Anderson sisters performing tonight?"

But before Tune Ann could swallow and answer, the color TV, standing sentry in Emma's grand living room, told her everything she needed to know about her daughters. Right there in Technicolor, for the entire world to see, were Sister, Sparkle and Dolores, sauntering onto the stage

of the Fillmore, taking their places at microphones behind
the emcee.

"Ladies and gentlemen," the host announced. "Live at
the Fillmore Theater, please help me welcome . . . Sister
and Her Sisters!"

Shocked, Emma slid the phone from her ear, down the
side of her face, down the front of her chest and finally,
brought it to a rest at her side. "I'll be damned," she said
simply.

Sparkle, Sister and Dolores hadn't said a word while they
stood in the wings of the Fillmore stage; the two eldest of
the three were both too mad to say anything, and Sparkle
was too busy trying to let the words Stix had said in the
quick prayer he gave over the group before the stage manager trotted them out of the dressing room wash over her
mind and settle her nerves. "Bless them, Lord," Stix said,
with the fire of a preacher. "Help them to show up and
show out on that stage like never before so that the world
will know the power and the beauty and the talent of Sister
and Her Sisters."

And when the announcer called their names and they
made it to the stage and leaned into those microphones
and waited to hear the first keys of "Hooked on Your
Love" as their eyes swept over the massive, packed theater, Sparkle knew right there, on that stage, that she was
born to shine.

Sister wasted no time drawing in the audience. Her
voice was like a one-two punch to the gut—clear, strong

and biting. She flowed like water across the stage, her breasts, her hips, the way she moved her hands drawing every eye to her as she delivered Sparkle's songs to the packed crowd. Sparkle and Dolores's crisp harmonies were nothing short of perfection—the perfect complement as Sister motored through their selections, pouring on her sexy charm with every note.

Stix could hardly contain himself as he watched the women from the third row. He had the perfect view of the show and, more importantly, of the record executives who'd come that night. They were there to see Aretha perform, sure, but Stix knew that once they got a gander of Sister and Her Sisters, they would be fist-fighting to see who could get them signed to their record label first. Stix had his eye on Berry Gordy, who was nodding his head to the beat as he watched the show. "That's right," Stix said to himself. "It's great music. You like that, don't you, Berry?" That was exactly what Stix hoped.

But it was Larry Robinson, an executive from Columbia Records, who made Stix believe he could leave the Fillmore with something solid for Sister and Her Sisters. Larry, stationed in the front row, was leaning into the stage, staring at Sister like he was going jump up there and take a bite. "Yeah," Stix said to himself, nodding. "I got you, don't I, Mr. Robinson? I got you."

It was the chords of a song Stix had never heard before that swayed his attention from the executives and back to the stage. Sister, Sparkle and Dolores had gathered close together, their bodies practically breast to back, and started swaying and gyrating as one to a slow, sexy piano rhythm

accented by the tapping of the snare. The three simulta-
neously dipped down and sang "shoo-doop" in a perfect,
tight harmony over their bare shoulders, tossing their hair
for added effect, a move that enticed every eye in the house.
And when the words dripped from Sister's lips—"Many
say that I'm too young/To let you know just where I'm coming from/But you will see, it's just a matter of time/My love
will surely make you mine"—everybody in the house was
leaning forward in their seats, their breathing suspended
as the passion and sentiment of the song enveloped them.

Sparkle spotted Stix and trained her eyes on his as she
powered through the chorus: "Giving him something he
can feel/To let him know this love is real," she sang as she
swayed sexily to the beat. She wasn't scared. She wasn't
nervous. Damn for sure wasn't shy. Her hips, her hands,
her pout, her fingers in her hair—every ounce of her being
oozed for Stix. Right there on that stage, she became a
woman right before his eyes.

*Damn, she wrote the hell out of that song*, Stix laughed
to himself. He took a long gulp as he leaned in toward the
stage, his eyes making it clear that he wanted more. Her
seduction was so explicit, Stix had to loosen his tie. Watching her gyrate and purr just for him felt almost better than
sex. Almost.

Sparkle tossed Stix a seductive grin as Sister moved
toward the foot of the stage and seductively worked the
crowd like she never had before. For just a split second,
she saw Satin, down in the front watching intensely as
she commanded the stage, the fresh scar she'd put on his
face glistening in the floodlights. "Nothing's wrong, it's all

right/My man," she sang before switching to the other side of the stage to swing and tease the crowd.

Everyone in the room, from the record executives and the Fillmore manager to the ticket collectors and the janitor who cleaned up after the crowd, knew they were watching a life-changing moment for the girls, and every last one of them loved bearing witness to it. And when they hit their last note, the crowd rushed to their feet to give Sister and Her Sisters the ovation they craved. The ovation they deserved.

Hours later, while Sister, Sparkle and Dolores were still riding high as fellow performers, wannabes and all manner of beautiful people mingled at the after party in the Fillmore Bar and Lounge, each of them doing their best to get close to the girls' table to extend their regards and say congratulations. The sisters greeted people with excitement, but a cloud—heavy, dreary—hung over them. Yes, they'd had a night to remember, but they were worried about what was to come in the morning.

Stix, oblivious, bounced up to them with a gentleman the women didn't recognize in tow. "Ladies, I want you to meet Larry Robinson of Columbia Records."

"Hi," they said in unison.

"Oh, look at that, they say 'hi' in harmony," Mr. Robinson laughed.

Dolores frowned and turned her attention to Stix. "Didn't you say something about Berry Gordy?" she asked. "No offense, Mr. Robinson."

Larry smiled. "None taken."

"Dee, Mr. Robinson is a senior A and R at Columbia in

Los Angeles," Stix said, smiling. That Dolores was a smart one, he surmised. Mention Berry in front of Columbia and Larry is on the defensive. Excited. Dee was good. Really good. "He's set up an office here to find some talent. He wants to talk to us about a record."

"Can I share it?" Larry interrupted. "Will you let it be my news?"

"By all means," Stix said.

"You were fantastic. Fan-tas-stic!" Larry said excitedly. "I want to sign you. I'm going to sign you. Let me go back to my first thought—want to sign you. But because I'm an impulsive guy, I can't. I have to stop and count to twenty. Not literally, but here's the deal: I got to see what you look like waking up next to me in the morning."

"Stix, what is this?" Dolores said, reeling.

"It's an expression," Larry said quickly to ease the misunderstanding. "I need to see you in the light of day— another expression. Look, the point is I need to see you again before I sign you. It'll be fun. You'll get dolled up, prepare a new song, I'll invite some of my colleagues and you wow us." He turned his attention to Sister: "It's all your fault. I'm not sure if you guys can really sing or if I just couldn't keep my eyes off you."

Larry stepped in closer to Sister, but she turned her face away so that he couldn't get a good look at her bruises.

"Oh, you're a coy one. I like that. It works on many levels," Larry said before turning his attention to Stix. Sister said nothing—just casually flipped her hair into her face and kept her head down. "Great, so I'll see you next week," Larry said, intrigued.

Larry was still staring at Sister when he turned to leave, which was why he didn't see that Satin was standing right behind him. Larry crashed right into him. "Wow, there's a line to get in here," Larry said, his eyes settling on the deep gash on Satin's face. "Excuse me."

Stix waved at Larry and crossed over to shake Satin's hand. "Your lady was, once again, incredible," he said.

"You all were," Satin said smoothly. "Congratulations."

Sister shifted from one foot to the other and barely looked up; neither Sparkle nor Dolores responded. Stix noticed the tension, but the fresh scar on Satin's face distracted him.

"You been fighting?" Stix asked, frowning as he surveyed the gash.

"I got a new cat," Satin said simply.

"That's a big-ass cat," Stix said, leaning in to get a closer look. He turned his attention back to the girls. "You guys better get out of here. The car is up front," he added as he walked over to Sparkle and leaned into her ear. "I saw you up there singing to me, teasing me," he whispered.

"You said you wanted better songs, something hot," Sparkle said coyly.

"Girl, you better stop," he said as he pressed his lips against hers. It was quick, but the passion that passed between them was electric. "You guys were incredible, but I have to run and see if I can talk to Berry and get us a bidding war," he said after he pulled back. "Satin," Stix said, nodding.

"Stix," Satin nodded back.

When Stix was fully out of sight, Satin turned his attention back to the ladies. "Come on, baby, let's go celebrate," he said.

Sister started to get up from her chair, but Sparkle and Dolores quickly, instinctively, stood between them. He wasn't going anywhere with their sister. Not if they had anything to do with it.

"What? Y'all her bodyguards now?" he chuckled.

"We're big-ass cats," Dolores sneered.

Satin stared Dolores down, but she didn't budge. His menacing glare did scare her a bit, though. He was a monster, that much was clear, and she didn't want to tangle with him. But she didn't want her sister to, either.

"I'll wait for you by the bar," Satin said to Sister, even though he was still staring at Dolores.

When he was far enough away, Dolores grabbed Sister's hand and pulled her out of the chair. "Come on, let's get out of here," she said. "Mom will let you back in the house."

"You guys, really," Sister said, pulling her hand away. "I fell."

"You said Mom used to fall a lot, too," Dolores snapped. "You even picked her up a few times."

"It was one time," Sister said.

"Too many," Sparkle said, finding he voice. "Sister, look at me."

Sister refused.

"Tammy!" Sparkle called out.

That got her attention. Sister looked up. "Don't call me that," she snapped.

"Look," Sparkle said. "I know I don't remember when we lived in the projects, but I do know a rat when I see one.

And he's just going to drag you into the gutter with him."
Sparkle held out her hand. "Walk out of here with us."

Sister let Sparkle's hand hang for a long time before she
reluctantly reached for her fingers.

The two, with Dolores bringing up the rear, walked
toward the door and had almost made it out when Sister
looked across the room and saw Satin holding court—
laughing and sipping champagne. As if he could feel Sister
looking at him, Satin turned in her direction and raised his
glass in a subtle toast to her and smiled. Sister smiled back.
And as she took him in—his suit, his smile—as she heard
the words he'd whispered in her ear earlier that morning
when they made love—"I'll never hurt you again," he promised. "You're my heart. My joy. I don't want to ever lose
you."—she gently slipped her hand out of Sparkle's and,
without looking at her sisters, headed in Satin's direction.

Time stood still as Sparkle and Dolores watched their
sister disappear into the crowd.

Sparkle and Dolores didn't say another word—not
while they walked out of the theater, not while they rode
home in the car, not even while they took off their shoes
and tiptoed into the house. Sparkle was so concerned with
closing the front door without making too much noise, she
almost didn't notice the suitcases sitting in the foyer. Or
her mother sitting on the couch.

"Mama, I'm sorry," Dolores said quietly, shaking her
head.

"I'm sorry, too," Sparkle whispered.

Emma, her arms folded across her chest, wasn't trying
to hear it. "Was my life not enough of a cautionary tale for

you?" she demanded. "You think I'm just a mean mama, I won't let you follow your dreams. Well, then I'll be mean, because I will never encourage you to drive your life right into hell!"

"To be honest, I can take it or leave it," Dolores said matter-of-factly. "But we are close to getting a record deal. They're saying Sister could be like Diana Ross and Sparkle could be the next Smokey Robinson, as far as songwriting goes."

Emma had heard this all before. Practically word for word. There was always someone out there willing to fill a girl's head with big dreams—to package her in a sexy dress and let her work the stage for pennies while everyone fed off of her hard work. What no one realized until it was too late, though, was that when the lights dimmed and the crowd quieted, girls like hers were always left with nothing but broken dreams, shattered hearts and tragic memories of abuse—abuse at the hands of careless handlers and greedy managers. Men who insisted they loved them, until their shine became too bright for jealous eyes. Even the pennies would be gone. She couldn't stand around and see her daughters suffer the same fate as she—couldn't stand that they just wouldn't listen to their mama and stay far, far away from "the business." She couldn't in good conscience watch them repeat her mistakes. Going down that road nearly killed her—nearly cost Emma her life. Her family. She didn't have it in her to fight again.

"I made it real simple in this house," Emma said. "Respect, education and having a relationship with the Lord. You can't do that, it's time to go."

For Dolores, Emma's ultimatum was a pretty simple one to meet; she wanted to go to school and become a doctor. Singing was a means to that end; she could always find another way to scrape up the cash she needed for her classes. But to Sparkle, being told she had to choose between her family and her music was like telling her she had to choose between breathing and her heart beating. One could not exist without the other. And Sparkle didn't want them to.

"Why would the Lord give me this gift if I wasn't supposed to use it?" Sparkle whispered.

"What?" Emma snapped.

"All I think about is music," Sparkle aid. "Everything I hear, see, feel, turns into a song. Sometimes I try to turn it off, but I can't. And I know the Lord loves me and He wouldn't torture me with something I want to do, can't help but do. So I figured . . ."

"That I was wrong?" Emma interrupted.

"That I had a gift," Sparkle said, her voice getting stronger.

"You can have a gift," Emma said. "It's how you use it. You want to promote good, or promote more fast-tailed girls having illegitimate children?"

Emma, still hot from watching her daughters on TV—*national TV!*—slinking across the stage in revealing dresses, snatched Sparkle's journal off the coffee table and screamed the words that were on the page. "'Giving him something he can feel! To let him know this love is real!'"

"Mama, that's private," Sparkle pleaded.

"No, it's trash," Emma said, tossing the journal into the garbage can.

"No it's not," Sparkle insisted, shaking uncontrollably. "We were wrong for disrespecting you and the rules of your house. So if you want me to go, I'll go. But I can't stop now, Mama. I'm too close."

Emma caught sight of Sparkle's hand shaking uncontrollably and then looked back at her and Dolores, disgusted. "Another little girl with a dream," she seethed, shaking her head. "Thinks she's going to be different than all the other ones out there trying to get discovered. Go to your little meeting. In fact, I want you to go, so you can see what I already know. You ain't getting no deal. And when you walk back into my house and want to stay living in my house, this little dream of yours is over, you hear?"

Sparkle nodded. Tears streamed down her face as she watched her mother stomp out of the living room. Never in her entire nineteen years had she ever defied her mother—or stood up to her bullying and demands. She didn't think she had it in her to do such a thing. But the sight of her journal in the trash and the rush she felt on the stage that night and the sheer euphoria of having a record company executive tell her that he loved her music gave her the strength. Gave Sparkle her voice.

Dolores gently put her hand over Sparkle's to make it stop shaking.

"I'm proud of you," Dolores said, smiling.

# CHAPTER 11

IT HAD BEEN a long night, that was for sure. Tired as Sister was after putting on the show at the Fillmore, as beat as her body was from pushing through the pain of Satin's abuse to entertain thousands for almost an hour, she came alive again after she made her way over to his entourage. Satin did, too. He was posted up by the bar, telling jokes, buying rounds, in his zone as the ringmaster of the circus that surrounded celebrity—a position that he'd seemed to eschew with every accolade Sister got for her performances. He'd all but stopped coming to her shows at Cliff Bell's, choosing, instead, to either spend his time at bars, drinking with Ham and his boys, or staying in at the house, where he'd sit alone, looking at his photo albums and guzzling scotch. It hurt Sister that she couldn't look out over the audience and sing to her man, but eventually she got over him not being there to support her. Singing had become a hustle. A way to make some cash. No more special than putting shoes on rich white ladies' feet at the department store.

She didn't need Satin's audience at Hudson's. She didn't need his audience at Cliff Bell's. And she certainly wasn't expecting him to be at the Fillmore—not after the hate he'd rained down on her just the night before.

But Satin had always made a point of inserting himself right in the middle of the best moments, and on that night—Sister's night—he willingly, greedily, shared the spotlight with his lady. "A toast!" he said, raising his champagne glass as Sister approached him and his entourage. "To my fiancée—Tammy Anderson. The love of my life," he said, grabbing her hand. Satin gave Sister a glass of champagne and snapped his fingers at the bartender, who quickly handed him a glass of his own. "Baby, I'm proud of you, and I can't wait for you to be my wife. To Sister and Her Sisters!" he added, to thunderous applause. Sister ate it up, and later that night, when they got back home, she and Satin did a lot of making up—the kind that lasted well into the wee hours of the morning.

It was the sunlight peeking through the curtains, shining on her face just so, that woke Sister that next afternoon. It was almost one o'clock; they'd slept half the day away. Determined to get some sun, Sister quietly slipped out of the bed so as not to disturb Satin—he loved his sleep—and deposited herself on a lounge chair out on the patio, content to pull double duty getting a nap while she tanned. She didn't know how long she'd been sleeping, but when she stirred and awakened, she opened her eyes to a flash of light. Satin was sitting on the ground, staring and smiling, peeking from behind his camera.

"What are you doing?" Sister asked, rubbing her eyes.

"I always do this," Satin said, taking another picture. "You look like an angel."

"Thank you," Sister said, sitting up and adjusting herself in the lounger. She pulled her nightgown a little tighter over her breasts, a little disturbed by the idea that Satin would be taking pictures of her half-dressed, without her knowledge. How often did he do this? What did the pictures look like? And where were they? Sister made a mental note to track them down.

Satin rested his camera on the small side table next to the lounger and handed Sister a notebook. "Will you please read this for me?" he asked. "Tell me what you think."

"This is some new material?" Sister asked, giddy.

"Things are changing," Satin said. "More black folks can come into the theaters. White folks don't mind it so much. I ain't trying to lose that white money, but I think this will help me bridge the gap. Get some of my black audience back."

The truth was, Satin was having quite the time connecting with his audience of late, and it was starting to affect more than just his ability to get a laugh out of his more faithful followers. The truth was, as the comedy clubs at which he performed started to integrate their clientele, the harsh and overly critical jokes Satin was telling about black people and the Civil Rights Movement weren't playing at all; white folks were too busy being annoyed that they were sitting next to Negroes to laugh at the black guy on the stage, and the colored folk in the room weren't happy about spending their money on tickets to see Satin only to be insulted—not even on a dare. It was a surprise only to Satin what would come of his career as a result of that dichotomy: the white clubs started turning down his dates. Comedians who weren't funny, after all, were useless in comedy clubs. And the more Satin saw his money dwindle, the more desperate he'd become.

"Ham got me a spot over in one of those black clubs to try this out. I need to know if it's any good," Satin said, waving the notebook.

"I'm honored," Sister said, smiling. Truly, she was. Satin had never asked her opinion on much when it came to his career, and though she wasn't privy to just how much Satin's bank account had been affected by it all, she did notice that the number of shows he was doing had dwindled. And it wasn't lost on her how his being idle affected his ability to get along with her. Finally, she thought, Satin was treating her like her opinion mattered in their relationship. Like she had some say in their future. The thought of it turned her on.

"I'm elated. Happy. Thrilled. Horny," she said, as she straddled Satin and punctuated each of her words with a kiss. Satin kissed her back passionately, but quickly pulled back, laughing.

"Now, please," he said, handing Sister his notebook. "You know I want what I want, when I want it."

Sister smiled coyly. "Okay," she said as she got up.

Satin smacked Sister on her butt as she walked past him. "That's how I got *you*," he said.

Sister laughed, then picked up his camera and took a picture. She flashed a smile at her fiancé and walked into the house, Satin watching her until she disappeared through the door. "Tell me the truth, okay?" he called out as she closed the door behind her.

Sister poured herself a glass of water from the kitchen sink and settled into the sofa with Satin's notebook, excited to dig into his jokes. She'd always thought him a funny man—got a kick out of seeing him on television, for sure, but especially enjoyed his quick sense of humor and wit in their everyday interaction. When times were good between them, God, that man could make her laugh. Something as simple as taking a shower or sitting down for a snack could quickly turn into a stomach-grabbing giggle fest when left in the hands of her man, who found his calling as a comedian early, on the street corners of Detroit, where he'd keep his boys in stitches as they did what teenagers do when they had nowhere to go, no place to be and no money to speak of. Sister had witnessed Satin spontaneously turn out an entire crowd while they had drinks or shared a simple meal. He was quick on his feet, and everyone wanted to be around him because of it. When you rolled with Satin, you were assured a good time and lots of laughter.

Imagine, then, her disappointment when she read through Satin's jokes. They were dry, stale—full of cracks against white people and veiled attacks against black people, too. The narratives leaned heavily on insult with no real point: white people have too much money and don't know what to do with it; black people are too lazy to escape being broke; black women who wear Afros look like men; black men are obsessed with Cadillacs because they're bigger than the houses most of them can afford. Sister was hardly amused, but then, she wasn't a comedian, either. She knew how to entertain a crowd, but only with her voice and her body—not by talking or making people listen to what she had to say outside of a song someone else wrote. So really, she surmised, what could she tell Satin about his jokes that was constructive and wouldn't get him mad at her? If he, a successful comedian, wrote them, wasn't he the expert? Much like Sparkle was as her songwriter, or Berry Gordy was at picking stars?

And besides, how would Satin respond if she told him his jokes weren't at all funny and he had to spend hours thinking up something new? What kind of frustration and friction would that cause between them? And how would it manifest itself? Sister looked over at the front door and immediately had a flashback of Satin punching her as she said goodbye to her sisters just a few days earlier.

No, telling him that his jokes weren't funny was probably not a good idea, she decided. She would tell him they were the best she'd ever heard because at that specific moment, in that space and time, she needed him to be confident. She needed her man to be sure of himself. She needed Satin to know that he could reclaim his throne. She needed him not to beat on her again.

Really, it seemed like a great idea at the time.

But Sister realized rather quickly the night of Satin's performance at the Comedy Spot that the consequences of keeping her opinions to herself would be much worse when Satin was up on the stage, telling stale jokes to an unforgiving, all-black crowd—notorious for tossing boos in the face of any entertainer they thought wasn't bringing his "A" game. Satin's jokes were dead on arrival—falling so

flat and hard that Moms Mabley, Dick Gregory and Redd
Foxx could have come up and personally vouched for him
and he still would have been booed off the stage.

Sister did her best to help out her man; seated in the
center of the club, she laughed the loudest at Satin's punch
lines—often alone. Satin pressed on, but in the middle of
a tragically flawed John Wayne impersonation, someone
loudly called out, "Insert punch line here! Because this
joke ain't got none!" The club erupted in the loudest roar
of laughter of the night as Satin shaded his hand over his
eyes to zone in on who'd fire-bombed his joke. His shoulders deflated when he saw who it was: Levi.

There he was, sitting in the biggest booth at the club,
with a couple of sexy women on either side of him and
an entourage of hangers-on, sipping champagne and falling out all over the table as if Redd Foxx himself had just
given them a private audience. Clearly, Levi was the man,
dressed sharp, wearing gold all over his fingers and around
his neck, sitting back in his seat like he was running things.
A shot caller. Sister noticed him, for sure. And Levi saw
her noticing. So did Satin, whose eyes shifted from his fiancée's to Levi, who was still chuckling at him.

Before anyone could see it coming, Satin slammed his
mic to the stage and charged after Levi. Lucky for him,
Ham and Sister intercepted him before he could get to Levi,
whose crew, standing with guns drawn, were just itching
to pull a trigger on the man their friend abhorred.

In all the commotion, Levi didn't flinch. "What?" he
said to Satin, the whole club leaning in to hear the drama,
even as they scattered away from the eye of their storm.

"You like my ex, but not my sense of humor?" Levi winked at Sister and gave her a little smile. "Nice seeing you, Tammy," he added. Then, addressing the band: "How 'bout some traveling music for Mr. Satin Struthers?"

The band kicked into high gear, playing a funeral march it reserved for comedians who got booed off the stage on amateur nights at the Comedy Spot. Satin held the distinction of being the first paid, headlining comedian to get rushed out of the venue by its unforgiving audience.

The audience was still screaming with laughter when Satin pulled away from Levi, grabbed Sister by her shoulder and headed for the door, Ham close on his heels. "Get the car," he seethed, making even Ham jump a little. Ham tossed a look at Sister and did as he was told.

Sister, wracked with fear, wasn't sure what to do. All kinds of scenarios cycled through her mind: she saw herself running, but then Satin caught her and beat her right there in the street, for everyone to see. She saw herself getting into the car and, while Ham drove, Satin holding her hostage in the backseat, delivering blow after blow while they drove slowly through the streets of Detroit. She saw herself running and getting away from him, only to realize she had nothing—absolutely nothing—but the dress on her back, the shoes on her feet and a purse full of makeup and a few balled-up tissues. She saw Satin at his place, piling all her things—everything she owned in this world—into her three little suitcases, pouring scotch on them and setting them on fire out on the patio. She saw Ham pulling the car to the curb and calling Satin to the side and telling him not to worry about tonight, that it was just a small test of his material and that every comedian had to perform trial runs of his jokes until they were perfected for a wider audience—an audience that already loved him—and so there was no need to whoop Sister tonight. She saw herself crawling back to her mother's house, listening to Mama say, "I told you so," and "I knew you'd never amount to anything," while she squeezed into a twin-sized bed with her nineteen-year-old sister, who, too, would be doomed to growing old alone and bitter, just like their mother.

What Sister saw was that there was no way out.

# CHAPTER 12

$S$TIX PACED THE plush beige carpet like a nervous fa-
ther-to-be standing outside the delivery room, waiting anxiously for the smack and the newborn's cry. His lady wasn't
about to give birth to a human, though. Instead, Sparkle,
Sister and Dolores would be giving birth today to a recording contract with Columbia Records. If they played their
cards right.

But they weren't there.

There it was, only fifteen minutes before their big
showcase in front of Columbia's top executives—the very
people who would decide if they could be the next Diana
Ross and the Supremes—and none of them were at the
studio, ready to go in and get that money. He'd told them
at least a half dozen times while they rehearsed, another
half dozen times as they finished and two extra times on
the weekend that getting to the studio early, looking spec-
tacular and singing for their lives would all but assure that
they'd walk out of there with a recording contract. But no,

they were all too thick-headed to listen to ol' Stix. Sparkle, Sister and Dolores just had to push it—just had to make everything more difficult. What could the three of them be doing today that was so important that it would make them late for their big break?

Stix shook his head and looked at his watch. Again. But this time when he lifted his head, there was Dolores, making her way through the giant glass doors. Alone. Sporting a new, cropped Afro. Stix's bottom lip fell down so far at the sight of her natural, Dolores almost saw the gums attached to his bottom teeth.

"What the hell is going on with your head?" he asked, incredulous, unable to take his eyes off her kinks.

"The man said he wanted us dolled up," Dolores said matter-of-factly, patting her hair for emphasis. "Plus, I need something low maintenance when I go to medical school. Haven't gotten off the wait-list yet, but I have to think in the affirmative."

Stix shook his head back and forth violently. "Not today, Dee. Not today," he insisted, running his hands over his own head.

Before Stix could get out another word, Sparkle rushed in, flustered—much to Stix's relief. "Thank God you're here," he said, running past the girls and out the glass doors.

"Where are you going?" Sparkle asked, confused.

"I'll be right back. Wait here for Sister," he said.

Dolores furrowed her brow as she watched Stix rush out to the elevator and punch the "down" button. When she turned toward Sparkle to ask her what was up with her boy, she caught her staring at her hair. Oblivious to her sister's displeasure, Dolores patted her Afro again and asked, "So, what do you think?"

Sparkle, clearly taken aback by her sister's radical new 'do, tried to be nice about it. "We were taught that if you don't have anything nice to say, don't say anything at all," she said.

"No, I want to hear it," Dolores countered.

"I have to go to the bathroom," Sparkle said.

"Don't avoid me," Dolores snapped. "Tell me what you think."

"I'll be back," Sparkle said again, this time more forcefully.

"I'll come with you."

"I'm just going to the bathroom," Sparkle insisted.

"Great. Then I'll watch you pee. You're not going to disown me," Dolores said, grabbing hold of Sparkle's arm and following her.

Dolores was admiring Sparkle's dress—a cute turquoise number with dark brown polka dots—and going on full force about her need to embrace her African roots and express black pride by refusing to assimilate and straighten her hair to make it look more like a white girl's when the two burst into the bathroom. What Dolores saw stopped her in her tracks: there, in the mirror, was Sister's reflection—bruised and battered. Broken. Worse than the night she showed up at the Fillmore with the gash and the black-and-blue mark on her temple. Much worse.

Dolores caught Sparkle's eyes in the reflection as the two of them stared at Sister, who was leaning over the sink, slowly applying makeup over her bruises.

"I told you not to bring her," Sister said.

"I tried . . ." Sparkle began.

"Not hard enough."

"I'm sorry . . ." Sparkle said.

"Lock the door," Sister snapped.

Sparkle jumped; her nerves were getting the best of her, and she didn't know how to settle herself. It was bad enough that she hadn't slept the whole of the night before; she'd stirred well into the wee hours of the morning, alternately rehearsing steps, reciting lyrics and wondering what she could do to keep her nerves from making her vomit all over Larry Robinson's shoes when they performed in front of the record executives. But when she climbed out of the taxi in front of the studio a full forty-five minutes earlier than scheduled, the last thing she expected to see was her beautiful sister standing outside the door, looking like a homeless woman begging for pocket change.

"Sparkle, I need you to do something for me," Sister had said, rushing her words as she grabbed Sparkle's arm. The look of terror in Sparkle's eyes said it all. But Sister had neither the time nor the inclination to explain anything. "Sparkle, focus, baby," Sister said, this time, more calmly. "Take this. I need you to go down to the corner store for me.

"Don't ask questions, Sparkle," Sister said, opening her sister's palm and shoving two crisp twenties in her hand and a piece of folded-up paper. "Go down there to the corner store and ask for Grady. Give him this list. And bring the bag back to me. I'll be waiting for you in the bathroom."

"But your face . . ." Sparkle started.

"Just do it!" Sister said. Her raised voice made Sparkle jump. And frightened her to no end, making her feel much like she did now in that bathroom, her hand on the lock, her eyes shifting from her angry sister to her broken sister and back again, unsure just what was happening or how to stop it from ruining their chance of a lifetime.

"What's going on in here?" Dolores demanded.

Sister didn't respond, but Dolores found her answer when she leaned in closer to take a look at her face. Dolores had seen this before—recognized it from the bruised and battered women she tended to at the clinic where she volunteered. The waiting room was full of them—women who caught the business end of their husband's fists, their shoes, their belts, for no other reason than that they woke up breathing that day. Some of them were mothers. Some of them were married. A lot of them were sober. But some of them were not. Clearly. It was Dolores's friend Francina, a nurse at the clinic, who taught her the signs: fast talking, giggling when there was nothing to laugh about, forgetting things, stinking, bloodshot eyes, dilated pupils in a lit room and pinpoint pupils in a dark one. All of them screamed, "I'm high." As did the sign that Sister was displaying right before her eyes—the out-of-it-and-can-barely-stand look.

"What else is he pushing into you besides his fists?" Dolores seethed as she stared into Sister's face in the mirror.

"Just stay out of my business!" Sister yelled. "I'm fine."

"You're just going to let him kill you?" Dolores asked.

"It's not that bad," Sister said, scratching her head. She was blinking slowly, as if was just waking up from a long sleep. Or about to lie down for a nap. She slowly brought her makeup sponge to her face and patted foundation on her black eye. "It's nothing makeup can't cover up. Sparkle, did you get that face powder I need?"

Sparkle pulled a small package out of her coat pocket. It was powder, all right—but not the kind you put on your face.

Dolores's heart pounded. "You give that to her and you're going to wind up looking just like her," she seethed.

Torn, Sparkle tried to put the tiny envelope back in her pocket. But Sister reached for it, her fingernails digging into Sparkle's wrist.

"If we're going to sing for this man, I need my makeup!" she yelled.

"I don't know what to do," Sparkle pleaded to Dolores. "She's sick with it and she's sick without it."

"Aww hell. Just give it to me!" Sister demanded.

"All you're worried about is getting that record deal!" Dolores yelled at Sparkle. "You're not thinking about her right now because you're so busy using her, like everybody else."

"That's not true," Sparkle said, shaking her head for emphasis. "That's my sister. I love her."

"Then go flush it down the toilet," Dolores demanded in a whisper.

Sparkle hesitated—much too long for Dolores's taste. Disgusted, she reached for the package in Sparkle's hand, but before she could get her grip on it, Sister snatched it. "Don't!" Sister yelled. "Give me that!"

The girls struggled, Dolores overpowering Sister, who, weak from her abuse and her drug-induced haze, was no match for the shorter but sturdier Dolores. As they fought over the package, a small glass smashed to the ceramic tiled floor and shattered into a bunch of shards and powder at the women's feet. Sister dove to the floor after it. And as her sisters watched—stunned, silent—Sister scooped up what she could and frantically sniffed what she was able to get into her hands.

Sparkle and Dolores's shocked trance was broken by a loud knock on the door. It was Stix. "What are you guys doing in there?" he called out. He'd pressed his ear to the door, trying to determine just what all the commotion was about. He could hear it from the moment he'd rushed in the front door, fresh off of paying a random woman walking down the street fifty dollars for her wig, which he was desperately trying to get to Dolores's head before Columbia's record executives got a gander of her 'fro and dismissed the group outright.

"Don't open it," Sister begged.

"We're rehearsing," Sparkle stuttered. "We'll be out in a second."

But it was too late. Their commotion had set off the receptionist, a tiny white woman with a huge bouffant who still wasn't used to being around so many black people, even if they were celebrities. She was already bothered that so many unknown Negroes were flooding the reception area, but she was doubly nervous when she heard all the shouting and what sounded like an all-out brawl coming from behind the bathroom door—the same one through which the pretty yellow gal with all the bruises and marks on her face had disappeared.

The receptionist walked up to the bathroom door with Larry. "They're in there," she said, pointing past Stix.

"Use the key," Larry said, standing aside so that the receptionist could pass.

She fumbled with a large set of keys, searching for the one that fit the lock as she moved past Stix.

"What's going on?" he asked.

"You tell me," Larry said. "My receptionist says your lead singer is beat up and drugged up in the bathroom."

"Sister?" Stix said, furrowing his brow. "She's not even here yet."

Just then, the receptionist got the door unlocked and shoved it open. Just beyond the threshold was Sister, disheveled and bruised, her makeup smeared across her face as in some kind of horror-movie freak show, leaning on Dolores because she could barely stand. At their feet was Sparkle, on her knees, trying to clean up the powder on the floor with wet paper towels.

Larry, disgusted, shook his head. "Like I said, I need to see them in the light of day," he said to no one in particular.

Sparkle looked up like a deer in the headlights; her eyes settled on Stix's, who looked . . . defeated. Stix threw the wig he'd been holding onto the ground. None of them needed to say out loud what was crystal clear: their big shot at stardom under the wings of Columbia Records was dead. In fact, if they ever made it back to anyone's stage, they were virtually assured that they would spend the rest of their performances serving out a life sentence on the Chitlin' Circuit, never to be seen on

Dick Clark's *Bandstand* or any other white TV or radio station, ever. That reality coaxed tears to both Stix's and Sparkle's eyes.

It was a woman's scream—piercing, searing—that snapped the two out of their trance. Everyone turned and craned their necks to get a look at the lady, a secretary, running around in the middle of the office, practically in circles, jumping up and down and shaking her hands as if she'd just touched something hot. "They shot him!" she screamed between her tears. "Oh my God, he's dead!"

"Damn, is everyone in this place going crazy?" Larry mumbled as he followed the woman into the office he shared with an assistant and the secretary. Moments later, Larry backed out of the office, shaking his head and clenching his fists. When Stix, Sparkle, Dolores and Sister finally were able to see his face, it was clear something horrible had happened, but they weren't ready for what Larry was about to tell them. Not by a stretch.

"They shot Martin," he said, breaking down into a blubbering, snotty cry that practically made his words inaudible. "They shot Martin Luther King."

Their audible reaction seemed to suck the air out of the room. Sparkle got to her feet and followed Stix, who'd headed to Larry's office practically before he could get all of the words out of his mouth. There, a small crowd of office workers and record executives—young, old, black, white, female, male, in charge, blue collar—leaned into the television, where all three networks had interrupted their regular evening shows to spread word of King's death and talk about his life and contributions to the Civil Rights

Movement. Dolores, who'd deposited the still-flying Sister on a chair in the reception area, arrived in the room in time to hear President Lyndon Johnson deliver his statement—something about rejecting "the blind violence" that had killed the "apostle of nonviolence." And when the newscaster switched to footage of Dr. King's speech—one in which he prophesied that he might not be around much longer to see his "promised land" of racial equality, Dolores lost it. Everyone let her be when she started screaming and grabbing at her afro and tearing at her clothes. But when she started pushing the white people in the office and sweeping papers and office supplies and photo frames filled with family pictures off desks, and got to hollering about "devils" killing "all that's good in the world," Stix grabbed her.

"Help me," he called out to Sparkle, who'd never seen her sister, usually so perfectly composed, always so nonchalant and matter-of-fact about even things that made everyone else want to burn something down, totally lose control. Frankly, she was as fascinated by Dolores's breakdown as she was horrified by it. "Sparkle!" Stix called out to her as he struggled toward the door with Dolores in a bear hug.

"Look, you all have to get out of here," Larry said forcefully. "Now."

Stix pushed Dolores toward the door and motioned for Sparkle to get Sister off the couch. "All hell is going to break loose, Sparkle," Stix said. The fear in his eyes was palpable. "Dr. King is dead. If Negroes rioted over a couple of brothers going to jail for getting rowdy at the bar, what do you think is going to happen to these streets now that the white man done killed Dr. King? Let me get you guys home. Now!"

Sparkle jumped when Stix yelled, "Now!" but felt as though her whole world was moving in slow motion. She pulled at Sister; it felt like she weighed 1,000 pounds as she dragged her, her jacket, her purse and her makeup bag to the door.

They rushed out into the night air, praying, with every step, that they'd find a cab to get them back to their homes— back to the places where they would be safe and could grieve for Dr. King. For America. For Detroit. For themselves.

Though Mama's house was only about fifteen minutes away from the studio, it took Sparkle almost an hour and a half to get back to their place. Finding a cab willing to drive Negroes anywhere on the night that Dr. King died was near impossible, especially with Negroes taking to the streets to tear up anything they could get their hands on to avenge the reverend's death. Stix had to wave a wad of cash at one brave soul to get him to agree to drive Sister to Satin's place and then double back to Emma's to drop off Sparkle and Dolores before driving him right into the middle of the bedlam in Twelfth Street. Dolores, inconsolable, cried all the way to Satin's place, begging Sister not to go back to the man who'd turned her out, and then cried all the way to their mama's house, too, repeatedly asking through her sobs what she was going to do to earn tuition money now that their chances of signing a record deal were gone. Stix had no words. He just wanted to get away from all of the girls—far away where he could think about his next moves. Maybe, he thought by the time he watched Sparkle disappear into her house, he wasn't cut out for the business. Maybe he wasn't hungry enough to eat the meals Berry Gordy had left behind.

This was what he told himself as he braved his way back to Sparkle's house on his motorcycle in the rain later that night. Sparkle was already sleeping when the sound of tapping on her window stirred her awake. There, outside her window, stood Stix, soaked.

Sparkle quickly pulled her coat over her nightgown, grabbed an umbrella for cover and snuck out the side door to meet him. "Stix, what's going on?" she asked, a little frightened by the look in his eyes.

"I'm leaving," he said simply, as the rain tapped hard on the umbrella.

Sparkle's chest heaved at his words. Leaving? Her man?

"And I want you to come with me," Stix said quickly, hoping it would help stave off her reaction. "We can go to the courthouse, get married, then leave, if it makes it easier."

"I hope that wasn't your proposal, 'cause I imagined something different," Sparkle snapped.

Stix hadn't considered the art of his proposal or Sparkle's reception of it; in the moments when he decided he needed to leave Detroit, all he could imagine was getting on a bus out of town as quickly as he could muster. But the bus wouldn't move unless Sparkle was sitting there next to him. That was real. That was a gift. To him, it didn't need to be wrapped in pretty packages with bows and fancy stationery with grand announcements. It was simple: he needed to leave and he didn't want to go without his Sparkle.

"Baby, we got to get out of here," he pleaded. "People are trying to destroy what we've built. You and me started this thing."

"We'll put the group back together when Sister gets well," said Sparkle. She was determined to stay. After all, everything she'd known—everything she'd ever loved—was right there in Detroit. How could she leave it? She couldn't give up now; giving up wasn't an option. "They wanted us once; they'll want us again."

"It's over," Stix said simply.

Those two words set Sparkle off. How could Stix give up so easily on her and Sister and what they'd built? "One minute we couldn't have the group without her. Now that she's sick, just toss her out?"

"I'm saying you can't just replace the lead," Stix said. "That's like The Supremes trying to find a new Diana. We have to start over. And not here. Detroit is dying. All these riots. Heard Motown is even moving to California."

"You're talking about going to California?" Sparkle asked, incredulous.

"I'm talking about anywhere we can live our dreams," Stix said, caressing Sparkle's face. "So yeah, why not California?"

Sparkle looked into Stix's eyes. She loved them—big as pools, piercing. It was as if he could see straight into her heart.

"I can't leave, Stix," she said.

"Would she stay and do the same for you?" Stix said, raising his voice.

"I guess that's what makes me me," Sparkle responded.

Stix couldn't believe his ears. He'd been so sure that Sparkle would come with him—would be his wife. And here she was, choosing her sister, and a dead-end life in Detroit, over him. It was hard for him to say it, but necessary.

"Then you stay," he said quietly.

"Don't make me choose between my family and you, Stix," she pleaded.

"I'm not making you do anything," he said as he started backing away from her. "I asked you to come with me."

Sparkle couldn't move her feet; they were cemented to the stoop.

"You coming?" he asked one last time.

Sparkle stared into those eyes. And finally, she shook her head no.

"Your mother really did a number on you," Stix said, disgusted. And with that, Stix walked down the stoop and out into the street, leaving Sparkle standing in the rain.

Her hair still glistening with rain, Sparkle had barely laid her head down again on her pillow when she heard a soft tap on her door. She wiped her tears as Dee walked into her room.

"You up?" she asked.

"Yeah," Sparkle said, trying to hide the tremble in her voice. She was unsuccessful.

"I can't sleep either, thinking about her," Dolores said, sitting on the edge of Sparkle's bed. "You too?"

"Yeah," Sparkle said, telling her sister only half the truth. She just couldn't bear to tell Dolores about Stix.

"We have to get her out of there," Dolores said with determination, giving her sister a knowing look. "We have to save our sister from that bastard."

# CHAPTER 13

WHEN SATIN'S CAR made a left and disappeared from view, Dolores jumped out of the bushes, powered through the front door, ran right past Sister and headed straight into the master bedroom. Sparkle, not nearly as bold but equally determined to rescue her sister from Satin's madness, fists and drugs, followed Dolores, but only after wrapping her arms around Sister and kissing her sweet face. "We're going to get you out of here," Sparkle said, cupping Sister's face in her hands.

Sister, unclear about what was going on and too wasted to care, took a puff of her cigarette and blew the smoke into her little sister's face. "Want a drink?" she asked Sparkle. "What you like? Scotch? With ice? Naw, naw—you don't drink, do you? I got some milk. Let me get you some milk," Sister said, stumbling toward the kitchen.

Sparkle, defeated, let out a heavy sigh as she watched her sister, thin, frail, hair unkempt, makeup smeared, disappear around the corner. She simply couldn't believe how fast and far Sister had fallen since the day she took a stand against Mama and left the house in search of her independence—in search of a new life. Sparkle had envied Sister that day—wished she had the courage to go after what she wanted, despite what everyone else, including Mama, thought was best for her. "She's so strong," Sparkle thought as she watched Sister march to the front door, bags in hand, with her man on her heels.

It turned out Sister was the weakest among them.

"Sparkle! Come on—I need your help!" Dolores called out, snapping Sparkle out of her gaze.

Sparkle snapped to attention and trotted to the bedroom, where Dolores was frantically pulling lingerie out of a huge dresser and tossing the pieces indiscriminately into an open suitcase splayed on the bed. From the looks of the open and empty drawers and an overstuffed suitcase, Dolores had already done some quick work getting Sister's things packed away. "Don't just stand there—get the clothes out of the closet!" Dolores yelled. "We don't have much time."

Sparkle spun herself around and headed for the closet, a meticulously kept walk-in affair that held rows of men's shoes, suits, dress shirts and ties, color-coordinated and separated by solids, prints, pinstripes and the like. It looked like a men's department store in there, what with everything hanging beautifully on wooden hangers and organized just so. Sister's shoe and dress collection wasn't as expansive, but then again, it was certainly bigger than the little bit of clothes she had stuffed in the suitcases she lived out of when she was staying with Mama. Sister had fine taste—her dresses always had a little extra something to them, a little bit of flair that the country folk who'd migrated up north to Detroit didn't have access to and wouldn't know what to do with even if they did. Sparkle certainly would have spent a little more time borrowing her sister's clothes if she were a few sizes smaller. Sister was always thinner and, even though only a few inches taller than Sparkle, statuesque. Now, all those beautiful dresses just hung on Sister's body.

Sparkle grabbed the shoes first and went to toss them in a suitcase, but was startled by the sight of Sister, sitting on the edge of the bed, smoking a cigarette, completely unfazed by the goings-on around her. She dumped ashes into her black ballerina music box and smirked. "You two are funny. You can pack the bed if you want, but I'm not going anywhere," she said.

Sparkle and Dolores looked at each other—Dolores with fire in her eyes, Sparkle with resignation. Clearly, they were going to have to take their sister by force, but first, they'd have to get all of her things. Sparkle zoomed back into the closet and emerged with Sister's performance dresses, the load so heavy and long, she almost fell tripping over the hems of the lengthier, spangled pieces.

Dolores caught sight of what Sparkle held in her arms and shook her head furiously. "She doesn't need those dresses! She needs *clothes*!" she snapped, tossing her chin to signal Sparkle to drop the fancy pieces and head back to the closet. Sister laughed and took a drink—she was sipping champagne in a scotch glass—as she watched Sparkle make her way back to the suitcase with some of her more understated dresses. As Sparkle struggled with closing the suitcase, Dolores snatched Sister by her arm. "Come on, we're outta here," she said.

Sister bit her. Hard enough to make Dolores scream in agony.

"Did you just bite me?" she asked, letting go of Sister to look at her skin. It wasn't bleeding, but Sister's teeth marks left quite the impression. "You're crazy!"

Pissed, Dolores grabbed Sister's arm again and expertly flipped her around so that her arm ended up twisted high up behind her back; with a suitcase in one hand and her sister's arm in the other, Dolores made her move toward the door.

"Don't hurt her," Sparkle whined, as she dropped the second suitcase on the floor and moved toward Sister's jewelry box.

"You didn't say anything when she bit me," Dolores snapped. "Just get the rest of her stuff and come on."

Just as Sparkle was about to grab the box, Satin walked slowly into the room and stood in the doorway, assessing the situation. He tossed a few cellophane packets and four glass vials on the bed and then stood back, his arms folded, taking in the scene of Dolores struggling to hold on to sister while Sparkle rifled through the jewelry box.

"They call themselves saving me," Sister said. "I told them I wasn't going anywhere."

Satin was the picture of calm. "Y'all better get the hell out of my house," he said in a low, menacing voice.

Sparkle dropped the jewelry box, her hands were shaking so badly. She started rambling, hoping she could make some sense of what was going on and reason with Satin.

"We're sorry we brought this chaos into your home," she stammered. "But our sister is sick. We just want to help her get well. She's not listening to us, but maybe if you told her to go, she would . . ."

Sparkle didn't get to finish her sentence. Before anyone could even make hay of what was happening, Sparkle was flying across the room—the result of the extreme force of Satin's open-handed slap landing squarely on her face. A small trickle of blood dripped from the corner of her mouth as each of them stood silently, absorbing what happened. It was that blood, dark and thick, mingling with the clear, salty tears flowing from Sparkle's eyes, that made Sister see, for the first time in the months that she'd been with Satin and suffered through his abuse, the sick person he really was. Without warning—not even for herself—Sister charged Satin.

"Nigga, have you lost your mind?" she yelled, alternately slapping, punching and clawing him.

Dolores jumped right in behind Sister, fists and feet flying as she did her best to hurt Satin any way she could. Sparkle even struggled to her feet and tried to help, though she was doing way more screaming than hitting.

With the three of them getting the best of him, Satin struggled backward into the living room, trying to guard his face and his private parts from the barrage of fingernails, open palms and hard shoes. Then, finally, he found his strength and charged the girls until they scattered around the room. Barely able to catch her breath, Sister swiped at her hair and went in for more, screaming at the top of her lungs as she lowered her head and lunged, hands first, for Satin's chest. Sparkle and Dolores took off, too, each of them intent on putting a hurting on Satin before he did it to them. A jumble of bodies, writhing, slapping, grunting, punching, kicking and yelling, rumbled around the living room, knocking over lamps, vases—anything in their path—until, suddenly, mid-swing, Satin fell to the floor. He just . . . stopped.

Sparkle and Sister looked at his face, contorted in anger and disbelief, and then looked up to see Dolores standing there, still, with a bloody fireplace poker in her hand. As they tried to make sense of what had just happened, Satin took his last breath.

"Oh my God!" Sparkle yelled, her chest heaving. "Oh my God."

Dolores stood frozen. Speechless.

"Is he dead?" Sparkle shouted, shaking her hands and backing away from Satin's body.

Sister gently took the poker out of Dolores's hands, but still, she stood, motionless, unable to comprehend what she'd just done. Dolores, who thought herself the strongest of the sisters—mentally, emotionally, physically—was too weak to move.

"You guys get out of here," Sister said slowly, quietly.

"No," Sparkle said, shaking her head. "We should . . ."

"Get out!" Sister screamed.

Her words frightened Sparkle, but snapped Dolores out of her trance. With the expertise of a trained doctor, she sprung into action, dropping to the floor and pumping the chest of the lifeless Satin.

"Dee, he's dead!" Sister yelled.

Dolores paid her no mind. She leaned in and gave Satin mouth-to-mouth, confident that if she just worked a little harder, she could bring him back and leave calmly with her sisters.

"Dee, stop it!" Sister insisted.

"He's not dead!" Dolores screamed, slightly lifting her head from Satin's lips to talk and then diving back in.

Sister got down on the floor with Dee and pulled her sister's chin to make her face her. A tear dropped out of Dee's eye. She knew the gift that her sister was giving her, and she understood the cost. In every way, she understood in that very moment what she was never quite sure of until then: that her big sister, the one whom she constantly fought and criticized as selfish and uncaring, had her back. And a strength unmatched by her own.

"Mama was right," Sparkle said, her voice piercing the moment. "If I hadn't been too scared to sing by myself, we would have never been a group. He would've never gone after you and we wouldn't be here, or . . ." Sparkle couldn't finish her words. She broke down completely.

Sister lifted her face to look at Sparkle. "I would love to hug you right now and help you understand that this is not your fault, but I can't," she said. "You have to go. Get her out of here, Dee."

Sparkle and Dolores slowly picked themselves up and backed out of the house as Sister looked down at Satin. When the door was closed and she was sure her sisters were down the road and far away from her home, she got up, sat on the sofa, pulled the phone onto her lap and calmly dialed the police.

"I need to report a death," she said slowly, assuredly, into the receiver after an emergency operator answered. "I killed my fiancé."

Within minutes, the home she shared with Satin was swarming with detectives, walking through the house, snapping pictures of their bedroom, the living room, the fireplace poker, the broken vases and overturned chairs, the suitcases strewn haphazardly in the hallway. Sister stayed on the edge of the couch, sipping on that same champagne and dragging on a cigarette—her fifth since Dolores killed her man. In her lap sat a stack of photos Satin had taken of her in their short time together—Sister on the stage, at their restaurant table, in the car, at the park, on the patio, by the pool, in their bed. Sister perused the shots, admiring how beautiful she looked in every frame. In Satin's eyes.

"Ms. Anderson, would you please stand?" an officer finally asked, standing over Sister. She gingerly placed the stack of photos on the sofa, snuffed out her cigarette in the ashtray on the coffee table and took one last sip of champagne before she did as she was told. "Place your hands behind your back."

Sister stared at Satin's body laid out on a gurney under a sheet as the cold, metal cuffs squeezed around her wrists. "Tammy Anderson, you are being placed under arrest in the death of Mr. Satin Struthers. You have the right to remain silent. Anything you say can and will be used against you in a court of law . . ." the officer recited from a small card he'd pulled from his uniform pocket. Sister wasn't listening to the words; instead her eyes were trained on the red stain that was stretching and yawning across the crisp white fabric. Satin's blood. It was all she could see, even as the cops led her out of the house, down the stairs, past the nosy neighbors, into the squad car and speeding into the damp spring night.

# CHAPTER 14

*THIS IS ALL my fault.* Those five simple words were the only ones Emma could conjure in the aftermath of her eldest daughter's arrest. First, they pounded her head, then stomped across her chest as Dolores and Sparkle sat her down on the couch, one daughter on either side, to tell her that Satin was dead and it was Sister's doing. Then, those words found their way into a mutter—low, deliberate—when, as Emma's daughters tried to console her, the news aired a story about her child, the murderer. "Satin Struthers, the popular comedian whose controversial humor about the Negro condition won him a wide and successful career with mainstream audiences, was killed today in his home in an apparent domestic dispute," the newscaster said into the TV screen, as if he were talking right to Emma. "His fiancée, Tammy Anderson, daughter of former torch singer Emma Anderson and a popular local singer in her own right, is charged in connection with his death." By the time the newscaster finished flashing mug shots of Sister—battered, unkempt, hair askew, broken—for every TV-owning Detroiter to see, Emma had snatched herself from Sparkle and Dolores's tearful embraces and locked herself in her room, where she screamed those five fateful words into her pillow over and over again. As much as it would have done her heart good to scream those words out loud, Emma couldn't bring herself to do it; doing so meant that she would have to explain them. Not to her babies. She couldn't bear the thought of Sparkle and Dolores carrying around her baggage—her sordid, tragic tale. Only one child was privy to the details, and look where that got her? A one-way ticket to hell—the same hell Emma had worked so hard to escape when she was a young singer, touring the clubs of Harlem and staring down the bottoms of empty liquor bottles and dodging the fists of her lovers.

Sister saw it all. Sparkle and Dolores did, too, but Sister was old enough to understand what was going on. She saw her daddy, Roger Grimes, the trumpet player whom Emma wanted to marry and spend the rest of her life with, seduce her mother with pretty clothes and jewelry and charm in the early evening and then, after a show, berate, belittle and, finally, pummel her over things significant and things incredibly small: she'd fumbled the words to his song; she'd shown up to rehearsal three minutes late because the babysitter couldn't find a ride to the apartment; she'd worn the blue dress instead of the red. All of these things were infractions worthy of Roger's ire and fists. He near killed her when she found solace—both physical and pharmaceutical—in the arms of Loren, the drummer in

Roger's rival band. Somehow, Dolores, but a pea in Emma's uterus, survived the brutal assault, but it took its toll on Sister, who was only five years old when she was forced to sit, cowering in the corner, and watch her father beat her mother unconscious. Certainly, Emma didn't want this for her children—couldn't bear a life depending on a man who thought beating her was fair exchange for his company and money. And so she broke up with him—left Roger's band, found her a new place, had her second baby sans the help of Dolores's father, and started her new career, out on her own.

She'd been doing all right for herself, too—found a small amount of success performing torch songs in some of the smaller clubs uptown. She even cut a record, and it, too, found its way onto the radio in New York and in her hometown back in Detroit.

But things being as they were for women in those days, holding onto that success proved elusive; club owners stiffed entertainers, managers stole their money, record companies made promises they had no intention of keeping if the bottom line didn't stack in their favor, band members and backup singers were fickle and bratty and refused to take ownership of an act in which they weren't headlining. Juggling it all while raising two babies alone was taking its toll. And by the time Emma was at her wit's end trying to piece it all together, there was Roger, with his sweet talk and his promises, offering to help and assuring he could change her life and swearing he was different. No more hands.

Until he was using his hands again. By then, Sparkle had come along and Emma's career had found its footing again and Roger was a proud daddy of two of her babies and half-willing to help raise Dolores when the two of them surrendered to their demons—he to his cocaine, she to her drink, both of them to their violence against one another. Emma thought she was doing something when she left their home and found herself a little studio apartment for her and her girls—thought she'd escaped his wrath for the sake of her babies. But there was no escaping Roger. Everywhere she went, there he was. And wherever he was, there was misery for Emma—the kind that nearly killed her. The kind for which Sister, by then a young teenager, had a front-row seat.

The kind that would haunt Emma's eldest daughter for the rest of her life.

Yes, Emma thought, Sister's fate was all her fault. And because Emma had buried her past so deep in the recesses of her soul, there was no one she could turn to but the Lord to ask for forgiveness and beg for her child's life. All of this, a normal person would have laid on the altar on Sunday morning. It would have been delicately placed in the pastor's lap or it would have found its way into a devotional or a testimony, where everyone who was listening could hear firsthand her contrition and her plea for prayers for her family.

But this was not Emma's way.

Instead, she stood alone in front of the New Hope Baptist Church, the cold, scratchy metal of the microphone trembling in her hand, lifting her voice clear up to God.

Whenever I am tempted, whenever clouds arise,
When songs give place to sighing, when hope within
    me dies,
I draw the closer to Him, from care He sets me free;
His eye is on the sparrow, and I know He watches . . .

Emma's technical prowess was outstanding—crisp and dynamic, with a pitch and range that was the epitome of perfection. But it was the soul, the heart, the richness of her voice that moved. In the expanse of one lyrical line, she reduced even the grown men to tears with the passion she evoked. She needed no organ. No choir. Just her voice and her God. And all those who knew Emma well—which was pretty much everybody in the congregation—knew by the end of her last note that the emotions she expressed singing that song would be the only ones to which they'd ever be privy. Prayers would be said on her behalf, because it was obvious she and her family needed them. No one had the expectation that Emma would ask.

But even as the entire congregation sent up timber on behalf of Emma's family, her world was still unraveling at lightning speed. With one daughter behind bars, a second, Dolores, was sitting by with her bags packed, ready, too, to leave the shelter of her mother's protection. When Emma walked through the door and saw the suitcases, her heart lodged itself in her throat. There, beyond the bags, sat Dolores and Sparkle.

"I love you," Sparkle said, hugging Dolores. "I'll let you two talk," she added as she headed to her room.

Dolores patted the sofa, motioning for her mother to sit.

"With all that's been going on, I couldn't find the right time to tell you, Mama," Dolores said simply as her mother sat to absorb the blow. "I got accepted to Meharry. A lot of it is covered by scholarships, but I have to go early to do some research to get them. I found out the day Dr. King died, and now I have to be there tomorrow."

Though every ounce of her fought it, Emma summoned the will to smile. "The haircut worked, huh?" she said.

"I guess it did," Dolores said, absentmindedly running her fingers over it.

"Maybe I'll get one of those Afros and get some good luck of my own," Emma laughed. She was quiet for a moment. "Congratulations," she finally said, fighting back tears.

"Thank you," Dolores said, stroking her mother's face. "Don't cry. We've done enough of that."

Emma forced another smile to her face. "These are happy tears," she insisted. "Happy that maybe I did something right."

"I always complained about how you never let us do anything," Dolores said, taking her mother's hands into hers. "Thank you for that kind of love. And sorry I called it something else. You'll never know how much your belief in me means. I love you."

And with that, Dolores kissed her mother's cheek, picked up her purse off the coffee table and her suitcases off the floor, and walked out the front door toward the taxi that had just pulled up for her. Sparkle, who was lying on her stomach on her bed winding up the black ballerina on Sister's music box, jumped up when she heard the car door shut. By the time she made it to her window, all she could see was Dee in the back of the taxi as it pulled off and disappeared down the street.

Dee never looked back.

Still traumatized from getting beaten and watching a man die, Sparkle wasn't ready to see her sister—not like that. She'd lost even more weight, and her hair, gone nearly a week without benefit of a brush, curlers or a hot comb, was frightful. Worse, when Sister walked into the tiny cubicle on the prisoner's side of the visitor's room, she could barely stand up, so weak was she from withdrawal. Sparkle tried not to gasp.

"So Dee left?" Sister asked Sparkle, trying to kick-start the conversation and draw her sister's attention away from her sorry state. "That's good."

"Yeah," was all Sparkle could muster.

"You know, it's funny, we always knew we would have to replace one singer in the group. Now you have to replace two. I know Stix is fit to be tied," Sister continued.

"Stix is gone," Sparkle said simply.

"You two broke up?"

"Yeah. He's in California," Sparkle said.

"When did this happen?" Sister asked, incredulous.

"The day we lost the record deal."

"I'm sorry, Spark," Sister said.

"It's okay. It wasn't meant to be," Sparkle said.

The two fell silent, unsure what else to say. Sparkle hated seeing her sister behind the glass, dressed in prison garb, looking confused and dazed, like a drugged-up, caged animal. She wanted so desperately for her to come home and be where Mama and she could take good care of her, keep her out of harm's way. But judging by the lawyer's outlook on the case, Sister had a long row to hoe. "She killed Satin Struthers, a very famous man who was liked by the white folk here," he'd said. "And she admitted doing it." Plus, they'd found a cache of illicit drugs in the bedroom, which meant that in addition to the murder charge, she'd have to answer to drug charges. No matter how many different ways Mama argued that getting her behind beat by that man justified a self-defense argument on Sister's behalf, the lawyer told her to prepare for the fact that her daughter might spend the majority of her remaining years behind bars.

Sister had spent the last few days wrapping her mind around that possibility. Being in that cage, banned from her family, mourning her man, with no access to the things she craved, forced to eat and sleep and exercise and crap and strip whenever one of the guards said to get to it, steering clear of the inmates who meant her harm because they thought she was cute or because they were Satin fans or because it was Tuesday and Sister was breathing—all of it was taking its toll, and it was everything for her to not go completely, impossibly mad. But there was no sense in going crazy. It wouldn't change anything—wouldn't bring Satin back, wouldn't give her back her career, wouldn't make her mother love and respect her, wouldn't bring back the fine and fancy life she'd been living over the past few months. It sure wouldn't erase her past. So she spent every moment of her waking hours fortifying herself as best she could. For the inevitable. She had no one to blame but herself.

"Don't come back here," Sister said quietly.

"Stop being dramatic," Sparkle said. "Of course I'm coming back."

"You do, I won't come out. It'll be a wasted trip. Because I'm not going to let you crawl up in here and die with me."

"I'm the only one who comes to visit you and I'm not going to leave you in here by yourself," Sparkle cried.

"I got in here by myself," Sister snapped.

"No you didn't . . ." Sparkle started.

"Yes, I did," Sister said forcefully. "This certainly ain't the time for me to be lying to myself. Don't you think I did enough of that already?"

Sparkle had no words. The tears in her eyes spoke for her.

Sister got up and coldly looked at her little sister. "Please don't come back here," she said forcefully. She yelled for the guard and then turned back to Sparkle. "I hope you hear me trying to save your life," she added. "Don't come back here, Sparkle."

And with that, Sister followed the guard, leaving Sparkle sitting at the table, confused. Frustrated. Helpless. Small. With Dee gone and Stix off in California, the only somebody who understood Sparkle and let her be was Sister, and now even she had found a way to leave her life—from behind bars.

After Sister's abrupt goodbye, the level of depression that settled in Sparkle's system was so intense, she could feel it in her young bones—was sure that the walls were closing in on her and she would go stark, raving mad at any moment. For all intents and purposes, she was an old maid with one foot in the grave at the tender age of nineteen. Her life consisted of these things: waking up, going to work, coming home, eating dinner and going to bed—in that order. She had no real friends to talk to, nothing beyond cursory conversations and the occasional Bible study class or church choir rehearsal. And now that Emma was claiming credit for Dee's "respectable" life as a soon-to-be doctor and turning Sister into the poster child for what happens when a child of Emma Anderson's doesn't listen to and follow her mother's rules, Sparkle got nothing from her mother but I-told-you-so speeches, barked orders and tough love. The only solace she found was in music, and Mama even tried to take that from her every chance she got. Sparkle could almost feel her mother's hot glares when she caught her humming a new, catchy tune she'd heard on the radio or getting too immersed in a magazine story about one of her favorite groups. Even watching black people on TV became a problem in Mama's eyes if they happened to be able to hold a tune and Sparkle looked like she was too into it. Like the one night when Sparkle was watching *The Ed Sullivan Show*, Diana Ross and the Supremes were performing "Love Child," and Sparkle made it her mission that day to have all of her chores finished so that she could watch her favorite group perform. Seeing Diana, Mary Wilson and Florence Ballard shining, enjoying what they did and doing it well, coaxed a smile to Sparkle's face—the first in a very long while. But rather than find joy in her child's happiness, Emma responded with contempt, and made quick work of shutting her daughter all the way down. Before Sparkle could even tell what was happening, Emma walked by the TV and turned it off, right in the middle of Diana and the Supremes' performance.

"Curl your hair, get to bed," she said simply, pulling her robe tightly around her waist. "We have church in the morning."

Emma said not another word—just walked out of the room, leaving Sparkle sitting there on the couch, numb, staring at the blank TV screen. Finally, slowly, Sparkle went into her room and poured herself into her bed. There, under her covers, her pillow wet with tears, she decided she had to do something. She didn't know what, but what she did know was that she just couldn't continue to live like that—that if she didn't make a change soon, surely, she would die. Surely.

# CHAPTER 15

$S$TIX LIKED CALIFORNIA, with its sun and its beach and all the pretty girls running about. He'd had just shy of two months to get used to all that rainbow dreaming in the sunshine state, and he knew that if he put just a modicum of effort into shadowing Berry Gordy's every move, immersing himself in the music scene and tracking down leads in the clubs where local singers and big dreamers came to show off their talent, he would have a few groups in his stable in no time. Stix was a hustler from way back. He knew how to get his. Even when there was little to get.

But there was something about Detroit that gripped him by the gut. It was gritty, raw. Passionate. And unlike the posh, glossy but tragically empty façade Los Angeles used to prop itself up, Detroit had brawn and soul. Also, it had Sparkle. And much in the same way he felt about Detroit, Stix didn't realize how much he would miss her until he left her.

That first week away, Stix spent his time tracking down a place to live—he bunked in a transients' hotel until he tracked down a spare room in the basement of a nice couple in Compton, where it was clean and, best of all, cheap—and by the second week, he'd found the clubs where soul, R&B and jazz acts rushed the talent show stage, hoping that Gordy, California's newest big-time music resident, or one of his A&R reps would discover them. There was some talent there, Stix wasn't going to lie. But none of the performers had what Sparkle had. The innocence of her lyrics, the depth of her musical character, the emotion she put into every word and note—all of it, hands down, made Sparkle's work soar over that which had caught Stix's attention in California.

And besides, he loved her. The moment that Stix reconciled that in his heart and allowed himself to really absorb it, he set a date for getting back to Detroit—for getting back to his lady—and dedicated every waking hour up to the time he got back on the train to Michigan hustling, knocking down every pool hall he could find to collect the cash he would need to properly bankroll the career of the woman he wanted to spend the rest of his life with. Stix knew that writing and performing music was what Sparkle loved most, and he made it his personal mission to give the woman he adored her heart's desire. He was going to make her happy, or die trying.

Within a month, he'd made it back to Detroit, cash in hand, ready to claim what he thought was rightfully his. First, though, he had to get settled; sleeping on Levi's couch was no longer an option—not just because Stix needed his own space, but because his cousin was still pretty angry at him for not coming to his defense when Satin was stealing Sister, the love of his life. In Levi's mind, it was Stix's fault that Sister ended up with a man who not only got her hooked on drugs, but ruined her life. Levi wanted no parts of Stix, and he made that abundantly clear to anyone who listened—might as well have erected a massive billboard about the whole messy affair in the center of Twelfth Street and back home in Kansas City. Though Stix had insisted it was just business, Levi did take it personal. And the two of them were no more. So Stix steered clear of his cousin and found himself a room in a tenement—it was only about half a step cleaner and safer than a homeless shelter—and took a few days to get his mind right as he prepared for the fight of his life: to convince Sparkle to sing for him again.

On the third day, Stix rose and went looking for the love of his life. He knew just where to find her, too: in a booth at the record store. He had to have been standing in that window, watching her lose herself in a Jimi Hendrix riff, for at least five minutes before she opened her eyes and saw him standing sentry over her cubby. When her eyes met his, Stix stepped into the booth.

"I'm looking for a singer," he said simply.

Sparkle took him in—all of him. He looked good—his skin had a cherry-brown glow, no doubt coaxed by the California sun, and he looked leaner than when he'd left. But just as quickly as she noticed the changes, Sparkle reminded herself not to be impressed. She was pissed at him. He needed to know this.

"My family is fresh out of singers," she said, fighting back the urge to suck her teeth.

"Sparkle . . ." Stix began. But she didn't give his excuses a chance to slip through his lips.

"When did you get back?" she asked.

"A few days ago," Stix said, dropping his head.

"A few days ago? I must've been out when you called. Or when you came by to say you're sorry to hear about Sister," she snapped as she started furiously packing up her things.

"I've never been good with sorrys or saying goodbye," he said weakly.

Sparkle smirked to herself. "You want to hear something funny?" she asked. "When you first left, I didn't think I would be able to live without you. Used to look out my window and wonder, 'Will I get through this second?' Can you imagine a person so unhappy they don't know if they're going to live through the next second?"

Stix tried to touch Sparkle's hair, but she caught his hand and gave him an icy glare that could have frozen Lake Michigan.

"Well, I got through the seconds and the minutes and the days and the weeks and the months, and now I'm doing just fine without you," she said, pushing past Stix and heading for the exit.

"You don't get to be mad," Stix said, chasing Sparkle though the record store. "I asked you to come with me—as my wife."

"No, you don't get to think that was romantic!" Sparkle yelled, drawing a few eyes from customers who were looking up from their record jackets and conversations to see what the commotion was all about.

"Sparkle, you want to lower your voice?" Stix asked, embarrassed.

"No, I don't," Sparkle seethed. "I've been lowering my voice for way too long, Stix. You don't just ask a girl to up and leave when you want her to. We talk about it, we decide together, then we go—you don't give me five minutes to leave my life to run behind you!"

"Listen," Stix sighed. "I'm sorry."

"Now you want to say you're sorry?" Sparkled asked, reeling back in disgust.

"I'm not talking about going to California," he insisted. "Remember that night I made you admit you wanted to be a star?"

Sparkle did remember that night. Every day for a month after he left her, Sparkle relived every second of that night in her mind.

"Then I told you that you needed your sister in order to do so. I knew I was hurting you, but I was so hungry to get something going, I took the easy way. Put a pretty girl group together—let Sister do her thing. I should've believed in you, Sparkle. Look, I saved up some seed money to develop you the right way and I came back to see if you would sing again."

"And what do I have to sing about?" Sparkle snapped. "Music ruined everything. Including us."

With that, Sparkle stomped off, this time leaving Stix behind. She was over it. Over him. Over Mama. Over everything. Over them all. And that conversation with Stix solidified for her what she'd long been thinking about doing but was too chicken to follow through on until that very conversation: she was going to live her life. To hell with what everyone else thought she should be doing with it.

As she made her way down the street, Sparkle reached into her purse and pulled out a folded-up newspaper she'd been carrying for a week. She'd snuck and fished it out of the garbage can the night her mother shut off the TV on her while she was watching Diana Ross and the Supremes, and whenever she had an uninterrupted moment free from her mother's prying eyes, she combed the "rentals" section, searching for a place of her own. She'd counted the money she'd saved up from her work at Cliff Bell's and the Fillmore and done the math: she could afford to move out of her mother's house and focus on writing music without having to be a slave to Mama's dress shop for at least three months before feeling the pain of not having steady income. There was one apartment, over in Twelfth Street, that she'd circled a few times; it was the one she knew could fit her budget for sure, but up until now, she'd been too afraid to dial the number and make an appointment to see it.

She wasn't afraid anymore.

Sparkle walked right past her mother's dress shop and headed for a telephone booth. She took a quick survey to see who was watching, fished out a dime from her purse and picked up the receiver. Two rings, thirty seconds' worth of conversation and a cab ride later, and Sparkle was standing in front of her new life.

The building had clearly seen better days. The landlord, an older white man, welcomed the wide-eyed Sparkle and led her up some dark, run-down stairs. "I have another building not far from here more suited for someone like you, but this is what you can afford," he said, opening the door to a one-room apartment. It had dingy sea-foam blue walls and one set of windows that faced the tar-covered top of the next building over. It sucked. And it was perfect.

Sparkle smiled. "I'll take it!" she said.

Not even a week later, Sparkle was loading her last box into the apartment, which she took her time decorating sweetly with flea market finds. Though she'd spent the earliest years of her childhood living in an apartment building deep in the heart of Harlem, when she referenced where and how she lived, she always conjured images of her mother's grand house in the suburbs. It was the white part of town, which meant it was quiet and drama-free—definitely after dark. The neighbors saw to that. But there in her new place, in the heart of the 'hood, there was always some kind of bustle—some kind of energy and movement. Sparkle loved it in the daytime; it was electric. But it did take some getting use to.

Sparkle gently closed and locked her door, hung up her coat and headed for the sink as she listened to the rush of cars on the street below. She filled a teakettle with water, put it on her hot plate, then pulled out a mismatched china teacup and saucer. While her water warmed, she pulled out a box cutter and dug into yet another box full of her things, working overtime to unpack and settle into her new place. This particular box was a jewel; it was filled with her used journals—the dozens of books she'd accumulated during the course of her songwriting days. Every page was full of lyrics—some with notes in the margins, others with hand-drawn doodles and pictures of things Sparkle adored—hummingbirds, fancy shoes, perfectly shaped lips, candy bars, fine cars, fingers intertwined. She ran her hands over the pictures and the words. All of them represented who she was—they spoke to her tastes, aspirations and the things that she wished she could incorporate into her life but had never been able to—because of her mother. Because she didn't have time. Because she thought that loving these things would make her the antithesis of what everyone else wanted her to be. And so she'd buried them in the recesses of her mind, or, more specifically, inside her journals and songs.

Sparkle picked up one of the journals and turned to the last song entry. It was dated March 7, 1968, and titled "Flying on One Wing." She looked at the notes to remind herself about what she might have been thinking when she wrote the four words and was instantly transported back to that night in Cliff Bell's when Sister, tired and defeated, put that poison up her nose, just so she could pick herself up enough to sing her song. That night, she seemed so . . . broken.

Sparkle pushed the image of her sister snorting cocaine out of her mind and unconsciously hummed a new lyric. The words "look into your heart" and "positive mind" danced across her consciousness as she blindly searched for a pen in the drawer near the small kitchen table where she was sitting. She scribbled the words, added a few, erased some and then wrote some more, smiling to herself the whole way. She was in her songwriting zone—a state of nirvana that she hadn't experienced since well before the big night for Sister and Her Sisters at the Fillmore. Her hands could barely keep up with her thoughts.

Only the sound of the teakettle's whistle could disturb her groove. Actually, the sudden noise scared the mess out of Sparkle. She jumped and then quickly settled, laughing out loud at how scared she was acting in her own home.

She laughed, too, at the beauty of discovering her long, lost love.

# CHAPTER 16

Do or die. That, Sparkle decided, was her mantra—the attitude she would have to employ marching into Larry Robinson's office at Columbia Records unannounced. She'd called his office at least a dozen times looking to talk to him about what happened with Sister and ask him to give her another shot, but he wouldn't come to the phone or return her calls. It got so that the secretary wouldn't even let her finish her greeting when she called: "Yes, yes, this is Sparkle Anderson and you're calling for a sit-down with Mr. Robinson," the secretary would say, exasperation ringing her words. "I'll give him the message. Again."

Sparkle suspected she did not. Or that Larry was avoiding her. Not that Sparkle could blame him; what he walked into that day when Sister, Dolores and she were in crisis mode in the office bathroom was probably still searing his brain. Tune Ann had even warned Sparkle during last week's choir rehearsal that Larry had put out the word that drugs had ruined what could have been one of the best girl groups to come along since Diana Ross and the Supremes. "He said that?" Sparkle asked Tune Ann excitedly as they walked through the church pews, putting away song books and picking up trash. "You heard him?"

"I mean, I wasn't there," Tune Ann said. "You know I don't go into the clubs. But I heard it from some pretty reliable sources. He was scouting talent down there at Big Earl's club and had a few too many drinks, and was talking all kinds of loud and wrong about you all."

Sparkle heard the words, but she didn't focus on the criticism; instead, she inhaled the part where Larry compared Sister and Her Sisters to Diana Ross and the Supremes. Sure, he was probably focused on what the group was missing and could never get back—Sister. But if he just thought about it a little more, focused a little harder on the rest of what made Sister and Her Sisters great, he would have seen that it was the music—the melodies, the lyrics—that was the meat on the plate. In that regard, Sister, while a beautiful and talented singer, really was irrelevant. Harsh? Sure. But true. The true star was the one who wrote the stories and made them come to life in the songs.

Of course, it was hard for Sparkle to convince most people of these things. Nobody ever paid attention or gave respect to the songwriter. Truly, they were blinded by the flash and glamour of the lead singer. The Miracles were exceptional with Smokey out front, with his pretty eyes and that silky, smooth voice. Everybody loved The Jackson 5, but it was Michael's pitch-perfect, soulful singing that made everyone notice them. Let the world tell it and The

Temptations were nothing without David Ruffin and Eddie
Kendricks. But what Sparkle was sure of was that each
of them—Smokey, Michael, David, Eddie, Diana—stood
on the backs of great songwriters like Norman Whitfield,
Lamont Dozier, brothers Brian and Eddie Holland, Nicko-
las Ashford and Valerie Simpson. And as far as Sparkle
saw it, she was a triple threat—a songwriter, a great singer
and pretty. If people would open their eyes and just give
her a chance, they'd see that. Emma included.

Sparkle's mother wouldn't hear of it, though. In fact,
when she used the argument to justify why she was moving out, getting her own place and pursuing her dream of
being a singer and songwriter, Emma got so furious with
Sparkle that it almost felt to her like her mother was kicking her out.

"I told you before and I'm going to tell it to you again,"
Emma seethed when Sparkle sat her down and explained
her plans, "music will be the death of you. It's not enough
that your sister is caged up like an animal for the rest of
her life? Or that Satin got carried out of his own home in a
body bag? My life wasn't example enough for you? Being a
celebrity will change your life, until it kills you."

"But Mama, you're still standing," Sparkle said. "Why
can't you see that?"

"Don't push me, little girl," Mama started.

"I'm not a little girl!" Sparkle said, jumping up. "I'm a
woman. Look at me, Mama! Look at me!" Sparkle screamed,
running her hands over her breasts and hips. "I'm not a little baby anymore or a little girl in the room dreaming about
what I want to be when I grow up. I'm a grown woman, and

it's time for me to actually be something. I'm choosing to be what I know God intended for me to be."

"God doesn't intend for any of his children to be drug addicts or punching bags or drunks or murderers!" Emma screamed.

"Is that what you see in me?" Sparkle asked quietly.

"It's all that will ever come from wasting your time trying to be the next Diana Ross," Emma snapped. "And I'm not about to sit around and watch it happen. No ma'am. So if you're going to run toward that fire, I guess it is best that you do it from a distance. I refuse to be a part of it."

Sparkle hated to leave her mother's house on those terms—hated, too, that her mother had refused to so much as give her more than a cursory "Hello, Sparkle," and the occasional "Glad to see you're well, Sparkle" in the months since she'd moved out. But in just that short amount of time, she had grown. Being on her own did Sparkle a world of good—personally and professionally. And if Larry Robinson wouldn't answer the phone to let her talk to him about her growth, musical abilities and mission to be a star, she would just take herself on down to his office to let him know in person.

Sparkle smoothed down her skirt—an adorable little number she'd picked up with the money she saved from eating nothing but oatmeal and soup for a week—adjusted Sister's flower in her hair and walked through the lobby of Columbia Records with her shoulders squared and her chin held high.

"How may I help you?" the receptionist asked.

"I'm here to see Larry Robinson," she said confidently.

"Do you have an appointment?"

"No," Sparkle said, trying hard to keep her chin up.

"I'm sorry, but you need an appointment."

"Okay," Sparkle said. "May I speak with his secretary?"

"I'm sorry, she's busy right now," the receptionist said, without even looking or calling to be certain.

"Okay," Sparkle said, turning on her heels and heading over to the waiting area to take a seat. "I'll wait."

She sat in that same spot for a good two hours before she gave up and left the record company's offices, but when the receptionist sarcastically called out, "Thanks for dropping by," Sparkle committed herself to going back the next day. The receptionist ignored her then, too, leaving her to sit on the reception area couch for another four hours. The day after that, she spent three hours in the reception area reading magazines. The day after that, she pulled out her knitting. On the fourth day, she alternately worked her nail file and wrote new songs in her journal, not caring at all that her loud humming was disturbing the receptionist.

The following Monday, she fell asleep in the hard plastic chair and was just a second from drooling all over her pretty pink blouse when the receptionist stood directly in front of her and said in her outdoor voice, "Mr. Robinson will see you now."

Startled, Sparkle opened her eyes to see the attitudinal receptionist standing over her with a scowl on her face. That scowl was no match for Sparkle's smile.

Larry was on the phone when Sparkle walked into his office and took a seat. He was droning on and on about an artist's album, acting as if she were invisible. Never once did he acknowledge her presence while he carried on for a good ten minutes. "Hey, hey. Let's just admit we wasted a lot of money. Salvage what we can salvage and make jambalaya out of the rest," he finally said, wrapping up. "Great, talk to you soon."

The phone was barely back in its cradle when Larry looked at Sparkle and said, very simply, "I have two minutes. Go."

"Okay then, let me not waste them on why I need you— that's obvious," Sparkle said. She had nothing to lose, so she went for it. "Let me tell you why you need me."

"That's a big setup," Larry said, still unmoved. "I hope you can deliver."

Sparkle rattled off confidently: "I'm beautiful. I can sing. And I write hits. Sometimes two and three a day. I've been kissed—twenty songs about that alone. I've been in love—another twenty-two. My heart's been broken—thirty. Plus I'm a virgin, so I have about eighty on what making love will be like."

She had his attention now. Larry swallowed hard and smiled.

"I don't know my daddy, I have a complicated relationship with my mother—tack on another fifty. I think the war sucks, flowers are pretty in the rain and it's really hard to follow your dreams. But you have to follow them because you just might write a song that will save somebody's life. I've got a great song about that—because right now, I'm trying to save my own." Sparkle finally took a breath, then added: "So can we do business?"

Larry was impressed. Very impressed. But he laid down

an ultimatum that, for the first time in the week that she'd parked herself in his lobby, wiped the smile right off Sparkle's face. Her assignment was Herculean. And there was only one person in her life who could help her meet Larry's request.

It took Sparkle forty-five minutes and a bus ride with two different transfers to get to where she needed to go to get to the person she needed to see, and she worried the entire way over there about what she would find. Sure enough, when she rushed into the YMCA, all of the men hanging out there gave her their full attention—an intense eyeballing that made Sparkle self-conscious and wanting to hide all of that which she'd proudly stuffed into the tight dress she'd intentionally worn to get Larry Robinson's attention. This kind of attention, Sparkle wasn't used to. She walked humbly to the YMCA worker at the desk, trying her best to ignore the staring.

"I've come to see Jeremiah Warren," she said.

"No women are allowed upstairs," the worker said.

"Can you call him down?" she asked.

As the worker dialed up to the sixth-floor phone in the hallway where Stix's room was, Sparkle tried hard not to be disgusted by her surroundings. Tune Ann had told her that Stix was there; she'd run into him at the record shop, gaunt and slightly frail, poring over the records and looking depressed. "He was looking for you, I think," Tune Ann had told Sparkle. She didn't really care; she'd made clear that she'd had her fill of Stix and didn't want anything to do with him—even told Tune Ann to cool it with the random Stix updates.

But today, she needed him. And by the looks of the hostel and the men who were staying there, Stix needed her back.

Five minutes into her wait, Stix descended the stairs, a scowl on his face. He lit up, though, when he saw Sparkle. He'd been waiting for her. Hoping.

"Hi," he said simply, coming to a rest in front of her.

"I met with Larry Robinson today," Sparkle said, dispensing with the small talk and niceties. "He says he's willing to come see my show, but I don't have a show. Figured I'd better get one. He says I have one shot at this."

Stix grinned. "Then we'd better make it count."

Finally, Sparkle smiled.

Stix looked nervously at all the seats that filled the expansive theater. He'd sat in the Fillmore at least a half dozen times and looked out over the theater from the wings once, but never had it seemed so . . . large. But if he was going to get Sparkle the showcase she needed to convince Larry Robinson to add her to the Columbia Records label, Sparkle needed to go big or go home, and for Stix, going home was not an option. He was invested in making this work for her—passionate about giving Sparkle her heart's desire. He told her as much when, after she came to see him at the YMCA, he convinced her to let him take her for a quick sunset stroll.

"Look," he told her as they walked arm in arm down West Grand Boulevard. "I was wrong. I was wrong about a lot of things, and I feel like it was my fault that things turned out the way they did, with Sister. With Dee. With you." Sparkle shook her head furiously, but Stix raised his finger, signaling her to let him finish. "I've had a long time to think about it, Sparkle. I've done a lot of soul searching. And the truth is, I was so hungry and so focused on eating that I wasn't thinking about the other people who needed to get fed. I never should have doubted you, Sparkle. I never should have allowed Sister to get involved with Satin—I knew what he was about, and my cousin Levi loved her anyway. So I betrayed my own kin. I never should have let you defy your mother or stopped your fight to keep your sister off drugs. Hell, if I was doing what I was supposed to be doing, she would have never been on drugs . . . ."

Sparkle stopped mid-step and jerked Stix's arm. In one swift move, she put her pointer finger on Stix's lips and shushed him. "Hush," she said. "Not another word."

Her kiss was everything.

And when he walked into the Fillmore, he had the strength and balls of ten men. That is, until the manager quickly brought Stix down a peg or two. He tried hard not to feel defeated, but to pull off the kind of showcase for Sparkle that the manager was insisting on would require a minor miracle and a day or two of Jesus himself handing out flyers to convince people to come see her perform.

Stix swallowed hard. "So five thousand and fifty seats. And the last showcase charged five dollars a ticket?" he asked the Fillmore manager.

"Yeah, but there were a lot more acts, and they all came with their own cheering section," he said. "You'll be lucky to get anybody to spend the time, let alone the money, to come out and see the third member of a failed group. But hey, it's still fifteen thousand," he added matter-of-factly.

"I'm talking about renting on a night that you guys are dark," Stix said incredulously. "You weren't going to make any money anyway."

"Still have to turn the lights on," the manager shrugged.

"And the light switcher costs . . ."

The manager didn't give Stix a chance to finish his sentence. "Fifteen thousand."

# CHAPTER 17

STIX HIT THE pavement. With a stack of handbills he had printed up, he went to every nook, cranny, corner and hole he could find in Detroit to convince anybody who could hear the sound of his voice to be at the Fillmore on Tuesday night to see the best show of their lives. "See?" he said, pressing the flyer into the hands of a group of brothers at the YMCA, "that's my girl right there. Her voice is even finer than she is. Five dollars and you can hear for yourself." He gave the same spiel over at the pool hall, where all the guys had gathered to win each other's money; down at Sandy's Grocery, where all the mothers were doing their weekly shopping; and at the Laundromat, the park, Sparkle's favorite hangout, the record store, at least ten different late-night bars and clubs that had talent shows popping and pretty much every bus stop in town. He even found his way back to church, and, after a quick post-rehearsal talk with the fifty-person choir, left stacks of the flyers with them to help paper the town with Sparkle.

There was one person, though, that he stayed far away from as he spread the word about Sparkle's showcase, and that was her mother, Emma. He told Sparkle that would have to be her burden. As scared as she was of how her mother would react to news that her estranged daughter was headed for the stage, Sparkle knew that Stix was right. She didn't want her mother to have to find out on her own or through gossip and innuendo that her youngest daughter was performing. Emma, Sparkle decided, needed to hear that news from her child.

And so there she stood, on the steps of her mother's stoop on a Saturday afternoon, when she knew her mother would be home cleaning up her place and taking in a little TV while she studied her Bible and prepared for Sunday school and church services the following day. Within moments after she rang the bell, there she stood, face to face with her mother, whom she hadn't had a decent conversation with since she'd moved out more than three months ago. Sparkle self-consciously patted her hair and ran her hands over her apron, part of the waitress uniform she wore to work at her recently acquired gig at Harry's Bar & Grill to help her make ends meet while she worked on her recording contract. "Hi, Mom," Sparkle said simply through a wide smile.

"Hi," Emma said. She didn't move from her spot—didn't open the door or smile or give Sparkle any kind of energy. Just an unemotional, curt *Hi*.

*Be strong*, Sparkle said to herself. She squared her shoulders and asked, "May I come in?"

Emma turned back into the house, leaving the door

open. Sparkle took that as a *yes* and stepped into the house, nervous and still unsure about what she would say. To her relief, when she rounded the corner, there was Miss Waters, sitting on the couch. She would not be alone.

"Hey, Sparkle!" Miss Waters said enthusiastically as she got up to hug her. "You look good," she added, holding Sparkle at arm's length while she looked her up and down. "A little skinny, but good. How are you doing?"

"Fine, and you?" Sparkle smiled.

"I'm always good."

"I came by to let you know I'm performing at the Fillmore Theater this Tuesday night," Sparkle said loudly, so that her mother, who was pretending not to listen, could hear her for sure.

"Well, you know I know," Miss Waters said gently as she sat back down. "Tune Ann is singing backup for you."

"I was talking to my mother, Miss Waters," Sparkle deadpanned.

"Did you hear, Emma?" Miss Waters asked Sparkle's mother.

Emma didn't respond. Instead, she kept her eyes on the TV—Dick Clark's *American Bandstand*. Sparkle was kind of shocked to see her staring at the TV so intently, particularly considering how much Emma claimed to hate the show. Whenever Sparkle and Dolores took a break from their chores to watch the performances and catch up on the latest dances, Emma would find a reason to make them get back to work, or, if they were all finished, spend the entirety of the show talking about how scandalous the dancing was, or how pitifully the people dressed, or how awful the lyrics were to whatever song was playing or being performed. But now, Emma was watching Dick Clark like he was Jesus himself, announcing the rapture.

Sparkle pressed on. "I have a flyer for my show," she said, moving closer to her mother. She showed her mother the handbill, but still, Emma refused to take her eyes off the television set. "It's my own concert. I'm not opening up for anybody. Just me."

Still, there was no reaction.

"I would really love it if you came to see me sing," Sparkle said, gently placing the handbill on the coffee table, right in front of her mother.

Emma laughed at something on the television, completely ignoring her daughter.

Sparkle's shoulders slumped. She felt defeated—as if she could do no right. Her mother had a keen way of making her feel low, no matter how high she was flying. But Sparkle had known her mama's response might be just the one she gave. It didn't feel good, but she'd prepared for it—told herself that no matter what kind of grief her mother gave her, no matter how many times she told her she couldn't do what she wanted to do, she would do it.

"Bye," Sparkle said simply.

Miss Waters watched Sparkle make her way out of the house and down the walkway, then turned her attention back to Emma. She was hot.

"How many times you going to keep making the same mistake?" she asked simply. Emma gave her the cold shoulder too—refused to look at her. But that never, ever stopped Sara Waters, her best friend since elementary school who'd been there for her during Emma's highs and especially during her lows, from telling Emma about herself. "Now, you can pretend all you want to that this isn't affecting you, but you and I both know better. You're a great mother, no one would ever question that. But those girls have to make their own mistakes, Emma. You can't keep using your mistakes as an excuse to stop those girls from living. You're killing them. And yourself, too."

Emma said not one word. She just focused on the window, where she had a clear view of yet another one of her daughters walking away from her. When she no longer could see Sparkle, Emma jumped up off the couch, grabbed her purse and ordered Miss Waters out of her house. "You don't have to go home," she said. "But you gotta leave here. I have to go," she said, pulling her friend's arm and pushing her toward the front door. "I got things to do today, right now."

An hour later, she was sitting in the visitor's room at the Wayne County Jail.

Sister peeped through the small glass window in the door as she waited for the guard to unlock it. There, she saw her mother, sitting by herself at a table—a sight she never imagined that, even in her dreams, she would see. After all, her mother had an unnatural contempt for jails and the people who occupied them, and had said to her daughters consistently that her shadow would never, ever darken the doorway of a prison, even and especially if it held flesh of her flesh. Sister approached quietly and took a seat, shell-shocked from the sight of her mother waiting for her.

The two women studied each other. Emma focused on the peeled skin around Sister's fingernails—trauma from Sister either biting them or using them to fight. Maybe both, Emma surmised. Sister focused on her mother's eyes.

"You look tired," Sister said finally.

"I am," Emma said simply.

"I'm in the middle of a card game and I'm winning," Sister said, forcing a smile that disappeared just as quickly as it came. "What do you want? Because I know it's not to see me."

They stared at each other even harder. And then, Emma's eyes softened.

"Was I really that bad?" Emma asked.

Instead of answering, "Hell yeah!" right away, Sister lit a cigarette, took a drag and blew out the smoke. It was too much time for Emma to sit in judgment; she couldn't take it anymore. But instead of getting up and walking away, she sat, stoic, and burst into tears.

Sister looked at her mom lovingly—a knowing smile slowly came to her face. "I always hated to see you cry," she said tenderly. "But I never tried to stop you, because I thought that was when you were the most beautiful."

Emma cried harder, and, through a series of ugly snorts, said, "Now you just lying to me."

"Well, not when you cry like that," Sister said, frowning.

The two shared an awkward laugh, but Emma still wouldn't look into Sister's eyes. She was vulnerable, but still much too proud to say what was in her heart. Sister understood these things, though. Instinctively, she knew what her mother was thinking and feeling without her mother having to say even one word.

"One day, you're going to stop worrying about what people think about you and finally see all the love there is for you," Sister said, cupping her mother's face and gently wiping away a few tears.

Finally, Emma looked up and into Sister's eyes. "You should get in the habit of taking your own advice," she said, swiping at her tears.

This time, Sister's eyes swelled with tears. And with every drop exchanged between the two, finally, it was clear to both of them that they were every bit one and the same— two women intent on making the world believe they were strong and independent and unflappable, even as those very things brought nothing but heartache, discord and ruin to everything in their lives that mattered.

"I love you, Mama," Sister said, finally.

"I love you, too," Emma said back. And when she said it, Sister knew for sure, for the first time in her almost thirty years on the Earth, that her mother did.

Stix sat alone in the house seats, watching the last flourish of Sparkle's rehearsal. Sparkle, surrounded by her dancers and the rest of the backup singers, including her friend Tune Ann, held her last pose, trying hard not to feel like she was gasping for air and about to pass out from exhaustion.

"Hold it, hold it, wait for your applause," Stix called out, his eyes sweeping across the stage to make sure they all ended exactly the way he'd choreographed. They were standing exactly as he'd envisioned. "Wait for your applause. Now go home, get some rest, bring twenty percent more tomorrow and be here by seven."

They all broke their stances, feeling pretty good about their work. As the dancers and singers made their way out, Sparkle, sweaty, crossed the stage to her towel hanging off the piano. She wiped her face and tried to catch her breath as Stix walked over to her.

"How you feeling? Good?" he asked excitedly.

"We can't do this, Stix," Sparkle said.

"Hey now, come on—have a little faith," Stix said, gently.

"It's all too much. Dancers?" Sparkle asked, looking around the stage and then out into the expansive theater. Exasperated, she sat down at the piano, a look of defeat on her face. "And look at this place, Stix. How are we going to fill this place? We can't pull this off."

Out of the corner of his eye, Stix saw Sparkle's hand shaking something terrible. He jumped on the stage and gently put his hands over hers. "You're going to be fine," he said quietly.

"What if I'm not? If I stay on the other side of this dream, I will always have hope and wonder, but if I walk out here tomorrow and fall on my face, what do I do then?" Sparkle asked.

Stix took a seat next to Sparkle at the piano and began playing the music for her song "Look Into Your Heart."

"Sing," he said.

"I don't want to rehearse anymore," Sparkle said, exasperated and shaking her head. "Plus, you're playing it all wrong."

Stix chuckled and stopped playing Sparkle's song. But he refused to let it go. "Close your eyes," he said.

"Stix, I'm not trying to be dramatic. I'm trying to be real with my . . ."

Stix put his finger on her lips. "Close your eyes," he said.

Sparkle did as she was told. And as Stix looked at her angelic face, he knew that the next words out of his mouth would be the most important he'd ever spoken. He was desperate to make them count.

"Spark, baby, you got to meet God halfway on this one," he said. "Don't see what's in front of you. See what He has already given you. See the place filled with people standing on their feet, begging you for an encore. See the sweat on your brow, feel hot from the blood rushing through your body, your heart pumping. See the smile on your face."

Sparkle visualized all that Stix whispered in her ear—and smiled.

"Now sing."

And she did. With her eyes closed, the words, lovingly, passionately, flowed.

When she finished her last note, and the sound of the piano finally faded, Sparkle slowly opened her eyes. There, standing next to her, was Stix, holding a small cake with a sparkler candle glistening atop it. Sparkle melted at the sight of it and beamed. She was speechless. And overwhelmed with joy.

"Now make a wish," Stix said, smiling.

Sparkle closed her eyes and took a minute to make a wish before she blew out the candle. "Ask me what I wished for," she said after she opened her eyes.

"What did you wish for?" he asked.

"That you would ask me to marry you again," she said, with certaintly. "But a lot better. And with a ring."

Stix laughed. "Did you peek?"

"What?" Sparkle asked, confused.

"At your gift?" he asked as he handed Sparkle a box.

She stared at the small package and then back at Stix, an easy grin stretching across her face as she reached for and opened the box. In it was a strawberry rock-candy "diamond" attached to a fine, blue plastic ring. She giggled, then looked back at Stix, tears ringing her eyes.

"Tomorrow, our lives are going to change for better or for worse. And whatever it is, I just want to be with you," Stix said. "Of course, if it's better, you get a better ring. And if it's worse, this ring will be dinner for the next few nights."

The two collapsed in laughter.

"See, even you aren't so sure," she said, finally.

"I'm sure. I've never been more sure in my life," Stix said, leaning in to plant a gentle kiss on his newly minted fiancée's lips.

When he pulled away, Sparkle smiled at Stix, then reached over to grab the lighter he'd used to light the cake.

"What are you doing?" Stix asked as he watched Sparkle relight the candle on her cake.

"Making another wish," she said simply.

And then she closed her eyes and, after a few moments, blew out the candle again.

"What did you wish for?" Stix asked after Sparkle opened her eyes.

"This one," she said simply, smiling, "has to stay a secret."

# CHAPTER 18

Sparkle twirled in the large dressing-room mirror and admired how she looked in the beautiful yellow performance dress Stix had bought for her showcase. It was lovely—short and just tight enough to show off her sexy curves. The idea of flaunting her body onstage still made Sparkle quite uncomfortable, but she understood it was a necessary evil—a huge part of her metamorphosis into a star. Plus, she looked good. Sparkle turned to Tune Ann, who was helping her get ready, and asked, "What do you think?"

"I think I'm proud of you," she said, smiling at Sparkle. "I think I'm happy to share this moment with you. And I think you look . . ." Sparkle watched as a look of horror waved across Tune Ann's face. "Oh Lord, are you bleeding?" she yelled.

Sparkle turned back to the mirror and caught sight of all that red, flowing down her face and splashing into a huge puddle on the front of her sexy yellow number.

233

"Oh God, look at my dress!" she yelled.

Tune Ann rushed for the door. "Somebody get me a warm towel!" she yelled. Then she returned to Sparkle's side. "Honey, we need to get your head back."

"Look at it—it's ruined," Sparkle said, waving her hands in the air and panicking, which made the blood rushing from her nose flow even harder.

"We have to stop the bleeding," Tune Ann said, dabbing Sparkle's nose with a tissue and trying her best to get her to hold her head back.

"Well, then maybe you can wear this one."

Those words—and the voice behind them—sent a jolt through Sparkle's system; she could hardly believe her ears. She spun around from the mirror at the sound of them.

"Mama?" Sparkle asked as she stared at Emma. Sure enough, her mama was standing there in a two-piece suit, with a full face of makeup and her hair tucked into a delicious updo—looking absolutely stunning. More beautiful than Sparkle had ever seen her. In her arms, she held a long silver dress with rhinestones that sparkled in the light. Sparkle, mesmerized, could hardly believe her eyes.

Tune Ann broke the silence. "I'm going to check on that towel," she said as she made a hasty exit, leaving mother and daughter standing alone in the room, feeling awkward.

"I don't want to get all mushy, okay?" Emma said simply.

"Okay," Sparkle said, tears and blood running down her face. She could hardly believe it, but that final wish she'd made over Stix's cake just the night before had come true.

"I just want to help my baby get dressed," Emma said, hanging the beautiful frock on a hook next to the dressing-room mirror.

"Okay," was all Sparkle could manage.

"Dolores always said lean back and pinch," Emma said, moving closer to Sparkle. As her daughter leaned back, Emma took a handkerchief from her purse, pinched Sparkle's nose with it and began counting. Sometime around seven, another voice pierced the room.

"Mama, it's lean *forward*. Lean forward," Dolores said, exasperated.

Sparkle and Emma looked up to find Dee, suitcase in hand, fresh off the bus, standing in the doorway. The sight of her second daughter made Emma's face light up; Sparkle squealed with excitement.

"Come on," Dolores said, dispensing with hugs and small talk and pitching in to help stem the blood and tears that covered her little sister's face. "We have to get this show started. I have a bus to catch in three hours."

While Emma and Dolores fussed over Sparkle, Stix was outside in front of the box office, chatting up the house manager as he watched scores of people make their way into the Fillmore. Some paused to check out the gleaming marquee, which read "One Night Only SPARKLE." There was excitement in the air—electricity. Stix could feel it, and hard as he tried, he couldn't contain his smile.

"I have to say, you got yourself a nice crowd here," the manager said.

"I told you," Stix said proudly. Sparkle is a star."

"She may be, but you have to tell me: how did you get all these people to come see a no-name singer?"

Stix laughed. "You can always count on church folk. There's 'bout fifty in the choir, times that by twenty, 'cause everybody wants to buy a ticket to see their child, grandchild, sister, brother, cousin, play-cousin, husband, wife, girlfriend, boyfriend sing on the Fillmore stage."

The manager shook his head and smiled. "Congratulations."

"Thanks for taking a chance on us, man," Stix said looking out over the many admirers who'd come to see his girl. Finally, his eyes settled on the marquee. "This is your night, baby," he said, the lights lighting up the pupils of his eyes.

Back in the dressing room, Sparkle took another look at herself in the mirror—this time, minus the blood and the tears and in a new dress, this one a slinky silver number with a deep, cleavage-exposing *V* in the front and a high split on the side. Emma circled her daughter, taking in the dress and Sparkle's makeup and hair.

"Beautiful," she said.

"Dang, Mama!" Dolores said, noticing blood on her mother's suit and on herself, too. "Oh no, I got some blood on me. I'll be right back," she said, rushing out the door.

Sparkle looked at herself in the mirror again. "You don't think it's too much?" Sparkle asked. "I mean, not enough?" she added, pointing to her exposed cleavage.

"If you're going to go out there, you have to give them something they can feel," Emma insisted. "Or at least get them to feeling it. Plus, Sister said to make it sexy, so you can't run and hide."

"You went by to see her?" Sparkle asked, shocked.

Emma's smile was subtle—replaced only by her tears.

"What's wrong?" Sparkle asked, rubbing her mother's back.

"Nothing. I'm happy," Emma insisted. "I always knew you had the gift. And it's not just the singing. You believed in yourself even when I tried to stop you at every turn. And that takes a lot of faith."

"Thank you, Mama," Sparkle said as she folded herself into her mother's warm embrace.

"Don't ever lose that. Some of us are still trying to find it," Emma said.

"Promise," Sparkle said. "You're staying, right?"

"Of course," Emma said, drying her tears with the back of her hand. "I didn't dress up for my health," she added, winking. "I'll make sure I sit far enough back so I don't upstage you."

As the two shared a laugh, Tune Ann barged in. "Did you change the music order?" she demanded.

"What?" Sparkle asked, confused.

"I'm going to go take my seat," Emma said.

"See you after the show, Mama," Sparkle called out before turning her attention back to Tune Ann.

"The conductor asked me if we were starting with 'Giving Him Something He Can Feel,' and I said I didn't know. He said he couldn't find Stix to ask him, so he was asking me," Tune Ann said, incredulous.

"We discussed it, because I wasn't sure . . ." Sparkle began.

Tune Ann cut her off: "You don't want to open with your new stuff?"

Flustered, Sparkle wrinkled her brows. "Where's Stix?" she asked, exasperated.

"Haven't seen him," Tune Ann said as she looked Sparkle up and down, noticing, for the first time, the new dress—specifically, the cleavage. "You look great, girl. A little cold, but great."

Before Sparkle could answer her, the stage manager shouted into the room, "We're ready for you."

"Oh my God! Where is Stix?" Sparkle yelled, panicking.

"What are we singing?" Tune Ann asked, adding to the pressure.

As she headed to the wings, Sparkle could hear Buddy, the Cliff Bell's announcer, onstage, welcoming the audience. "Good evening, ladies and gentlemen, and welcome to An Evening with Sparkle!" he yelled out to a thunderous round of cheers, applause and whistling. Sparkle, Tune Ann and the two backup singers, who'd joined them offstage, adjusted themselves as they waited to be called to the stage.

"Did you find Stix?" Sparkle asked Tune Ann.

"Will you stop worrying me? You're not the only one who has to go out there and sing," Tune Ann snapped.

"I can't do this without him," Sparkle said, shaking her head furiously. Sweat started beading up on her nose and forehead.

"You're going to have to—the curtain is going up," Tune Ann said.

"Places, please," the stage manager said as he shooed the girls onto the stage, just behind the curtain.

Sparkle's legs felt like two 500-pound blocks of wood; she could barely move to the center of the stage.

"What are we singing?" Tune Ann demanded as the stage manager counted down the curtain's rise.

"Five, four, three, two . . ."

When the curtain rose, Sparkle was sitting at the piano, shoulders squared, chin up, staring at her trembling fingers on the black and white keys. There was no fanfare—no grand curtsy or air kisses blown out over the crowd. Sparkle was too scared for that. Instead, she finally looked up and out over the crowd, taking in all the familiar faces—Reverend Bryce, Miss Waters, the Bible Study group, the choir, women from the usher board. Sparkle was overwhelmed with . . . joy.

Finally, she spoke. "I don't think I can express how moved I am to see you all here," she said. "So I will simply say thank you. And know that wishes do come true."

In the sea of people, somehow, Sparkle found her mother and Dee, sitting in the fourth row, looking up at her. Their eyes locked as they shared a moment—a moment that instantly calmed Sparkle. She leaned into her microphone and, with her fingers on the keys, said, simply, "This is for Sister. It's called 'Flying on One Wing.'"

Her piano intro soared over the theater—simple, spare, soulful. And when Sparkle began to sing, her beautiful voice bathing the lyrics and the music—just her and her piano—the audience melted. She had them in the palm of her hands as they swayed to the rhythm and leaned in to fully hear and understand Sparkle's beautiful words.

As Sparkle sang, the rest of the band kicked in to boost the song, and, with dramatic flair, Tune Ann and the backup singers emerged out of the darkness, kicking the song up a notch. But never did any of it overpower Sparkle. On this night, her voice was a mystic, converting souls. It was magical.

Stix, who'd been lording over the audience, gauging their reaction to Sparkle's performance, paid close attention to the way the assortment of recording executives were responding to her voice and music. He made his way backstage when he'd gathered enough intel on the crowd. His heart swelled when the New Hope Baptist Choir, 200 strong, emerged from the darkness and shook the building with the power of its sound—a riot of gospel soul that made the crowd go wild as Sparkle drove the song with her raw, beautiful voice. Stix was standing in the wings of the stage by the time Sparkle finished the song to thunderous applause. He'd never seen her so beautiful—her eyes closed, absorbing the moment, gratified. Stix was smiling and taking in the stage view of the crowd when someone grabbed his hand.

"Let's meet tomorrow," Larry Robinson said, pumping Stix's hand in a firm handshake. "I want to sign her."

"Sure, we'll come by after our meeting at Motown in the morning," Stix said slyly.

Larry smiled. "Why put off tomorrow what you can do over dinner tonight?" he said quickly.

The two shook hands as Sparkle got up from behind the piano and moved center stage. She put the microphone on its stand and leaned in. "Okay, now it's time to talk about my man," she said, beaming as she looked to the wings.

Stix was smiling and clapping. "There he is," she said, pointing. "Y'all want to meet my man?"

The crowd hooted and hollered as Sparkle gestured for Stix to step onstage. Reluctantly, he walked out and joined his fiancée. "He's a good man," she said, grabbing his hand. "I recommend every woman get her one."

Sparkle threw Stix a kiss and he sent one right back before stepping back off the stage. Sparkle leaned back into the mic and simply said, "This love will," a cue for the band to kick up the music for her song, "Love Will."

And right there, on that stage, in front of her mother and her sister and her man and her church and all of Detroit, Sparkle let herself go and sang her song with power, energy and a sexual intensity that was downright infectious. The audience rose to its feet, cheering, dancing and hooting and hollering for their girl as Sparkle claimed what was hers.

She was a star.

And this was her night.

**SIMON &
SCHUSTER**

# Then Came You

## By Jennifer Weiner

Jules is a gifted college student with a father battling
addiction. Annie married her high school sweetheart and
became a mother. India has changed everything about
herself and when she falls for an older man, Marcus,
she decides a baby will ensure her happy-ever-after.
But she must turn to Annie and Jules to help make
her dream come true.

Then each of their lives is thrown into disarray when
Marcus' daughter, intent on protecting her father, becomes
convinced that his new wife is not what she seems . . .

With her trademark emotional intelligence, Jennifer Weiner
takes readers into the heart of four very different women's
lives in an unforgettable and timely tale which will make
you laugh, cry – and think.

**ISBN 978-0-85720-812-5**
**PRICE £7.99**

**SIMON &
SCHUSTER**

# Killer Heels

## By Rebecca Chance

From the suburbs of Luton to the avenues of Manhattan,
starry-eyed fashionista Coco Raeburn will do anything to
be an editor at a top fashion magazine – even if it means
starving herself half to death.

Her idol is ruthless boss Victoria Glossop, top *Style* editor.
Nothing will hinder her ambitions – at least not until an
enigmatic stranger comes into her life and thaws the ice
queen in the most wicked ways possible.

Svengali Jacob Dupleix, media magnate and *Style* owner,
is one of the most powerful men in New York and London.
But is his glittering empire about to collapse due to a
dangerous liaison ...?

More cut-throat than *The Apprentice*, more glamorous than
*The Devil Wears Prada*, more sizzling than *Fifty Shades of
Grey*, discover how far *you'd* go to climb the greasy pole to
the top ...

**ISBN 978-0-85720-486-8**
**PRICE £6.99**

**SIMON &
SCHUSTER**

# The Perks of Being a Wallflower

## By Stephen Chbosky

Charlie is a freshman. Shy, introspective, intelligent
beyond his years yet socially awkward, he is a wallflower,
caught between trying to live his life and trying to run
from it. Charlie is attempting to navigate his way through
uncharted territory: the world of first dates and mixed
tapes, family dramas and new friends; the world of sex,
drugs, and *The Rocky Horror Picture Show*, when all
one requires is that perfect song on that perfect drive
to feel infinite.

Standing on the fringes of life offers a unique perspective.
But there comes a time to see what it looks like from the
dance floor. *The Perks of Being a Wallflower* is a deeply
affecting coming-of-age story that will spirit you back to
those wild and poignant roller-coaster days known as
growing up.

**ISBN 978-1-47110-048-2**
**PRICE £7.99**